NAMING the JUNGLE

THE NEW PRESS
INTERNATIONAL FICTION SERIES

NAMING
the
JUNGLE

Antoine Volodine

Translated from the French by Linda Coverdale

THE NEW PRESS
NEW YORK

Le nom des singes by Antoine Volodine © 1994 by Les Éditions de Minuit
English translation by Linda Coverdale © 1995 by The New Press

Library of Congress Cataloging-in-Publication Data
Volodine, Antoine.
[Nom des singes. English]
Naming the jungle / Antoine Volodine;
translated from the French by Linda Coverdale.
p. cm.
ISBN 1-56584-274-X (HC)
1. Coverdale, Linda. II. Title.
PQ2682.0436N6613   1196
843'.914—dc20   95-31883
CIP

Le nom des singes originally published in France by Les Éditions de Minuit
Published in the United States by The New Press, New York
Distributed by W. W. Norton & Company, Inc., New York

Street names in Puesto Libertad have been translated from French into Spanish;
all other names of places and things remian as they appear in *Le nom des singes*.

The New Press extends its thanks to the French Ministry of Culture and Communication for its translation support.

Established in 1990 as a major alternative to the large, commercial publishing
houses, The New Press is the first full-scale nonprofit American book publisher
outside of the university presses. The Press is operated editorially in the public
interest, rather than for private gain; it is committed to publishing in innovative
ways works of educational, cultural, and community value that, despite their
intellectual merits, might not normally be commercially viable. The New Press's
editorial offices are located at the City University of New York.

Book design by Ann Antoshak
Production management by Kim Waymer
Printed in the United States of America

95 96 97 98 9 8 7 6 5 4 3 2 1

NAMING *the* JUNGLE

I
THE SURFACE OF
THE WATERS

I

ONCE AGAIN the revolution was dead. Quite dead, in fact. I was ashamed of having taken part in that fiasco.

Yes, said the psychiatrist impatiently, you've made your point.

I'd started lying again, increasing the dosage of fiction each day, every night trying to forget, to shake off . . .

Enough, Golpiez! shouted Dr. Gonçalves.

He was waving some feathers around, a necklace of feathers.

Tell me something concrete instead of whining, he said. Instead of wallowing in stupid abstractions. You know perfectly well that death has no reality for us. Primeval inexistence, yes. Mud, yes. But not death.

Fabian Golpiez wiped his face with the crook of his arm. A sudden shower had drenched the afternoon in murky twilight. Now the air in the psychiatrist's office was even muggier. Sweat beaded on Fabian's eyelashes, the drops swelling and falling while Fabian tried to think what to say. Outside the window, vines were dripping dry, and in places where the foliage had recovered the dull color of old rope, creatures began to stir.

The revolution was returning to its primeval inexistence, continued Fabian. So were we. The sultry air turned stagnant, laced with scents of rotting vegetation. I felt changes in my body, my voice, my vocabulary, my dreams. I was slipping back into my true nature.

And what was that?

Now Gonçalves and his patient were both looking out at the trees no longer streaming with rain and the fauna creeping back into view among the leaves: little snakes, assorted iguanas, several kinds of millipedes.

At last I was becoming an Indian again, said Fabian.

Rubbish, grumbled Gonçalves. And stop all this chatter in the first person. Let's have no more of that.

The canoe, said Fabian. The canoe was drifting.

Go on! ordered Gonçalves, shaking the feathered ornament at him and rattling a tiny gourd filled with seeds.

Fabian couldn't see the surrounding undergrowth clearly. The combination of darkness and malaria was distorting his perception of reality, the jungle, the obstacles ahead.

He was advancing crabwise, carried slowly along at an angle by the pirogue, and in order to tell what had happened first, to return to the idea of birth or rebirth—back to that very beginning of the story Gonçalves so often demanded to hear—he described a spider web hanging across the river, blocking the way. He evoked the feel of the clinging silk, its texture on his lips, the hostile silence of the snare. He struggled feebly, suddenly prey to an unnerving anxiety, because instead of breaking with a soft ripping sound, the seemingly fragile threads that stretched vibrating from shore to shore refused to yield. He whirled the paddle blindly around in vain, brushing it against reeds and branches, stirring up a faint racket. Then something snapped. The dugout canoe glided through the water lilies and floating weeds, and now Fabian left ragged gaps behind him, a quivering wake sprinkled with pellets of animal debris, scraps of decomposing hummingbirds, stubborn twigs, insect fragments.

Fabian held his breath, still entangled in the huge web. He couldn't free himself. I don't know whether he was afraid or not. He'd fallen into a stupor.

And the spider? inquired Gonçalves eagerly. What kind was it? A caranguejeira? What species of caranguejeira? Size, weight? A janduparaba?

I'm trying to reconstruct what happened, Doctor, insisted Fabian, but I'm at the farthest edge of the memory, where nothing stands out distinctly.

A jandupichuna?

I don't know anymore, Doctor. I'm stuck at that edge in a daze. My nostrils are filled with fetid swamp odors.

So you were breathing, sneered the psychiatrist. Very nice detail, very schizophrenic to hold your breath in the face of danger. Yet you were breathing.

Yes, said Fabian. My nasal fossae received whiffs of squamous excrement, musty gases . . . I . . .

Hold it, Golpiez! Analyzing the stench is not on the agenda. Go on to the spider. A nhanduguaca? A tarantula? Was it crouching down in the thick undergrowth? Rushing out to attack?

Fabian writhed in his seat, in the dental chair Gonçalves had inherited from his predecessor, a dentist, and now used for the thrice-weekly compulsory sessions with patients sent over by the municipal health department. The old drills, the swiveling mechanical arm, the rubber tubes all danced about. The psychiatrist shouted, shook the armrests, and leaned toward Fabian, brandishing the gourds and the bright red and yellow plumes like a shaman.

I'm listening—talk! he roared.

And the suffocating heat of the office: like the atmosphere in the steamy depths of the rain forest.

And the psychiatrist's breath: like the smell at the edge of the worst crocodile wallow.

And from Fabian's armpits: new rivulets meandering down his sides. His belly was soaked. It seemed harder and harder to labor on, or even simply to size up the situation, to understand what was happening. I was rocking above brownish algae, clumps of duckweed. The surface was so thick with vegetation that no reflections glanced off the wavelets.

Wait a minute, Golpiez, said Gonçalves. Use the correct names for things. Duckweed, brownish algae. I'm quoting you. Sounds like the confessions of an imperialist tourist. Make an effort! Indian nomenclature is not just for show, you know.

My memory's gone to pieces, protested Fabian. Sometimes I can't find the right words.

Nonsense, snapped Gonçalves.

The shaman-doctor's white smock revealed glimpses of his undershirt, worn into holes, and his skin, worn into holes as well, pockmarked by ticks, insect larvae, and disease. His scrawny chest was constantly bathed in sweat. Fabian looked away.

So, the spider, insisted Gonçalves.

So, the spider, repeated Fabian meekly. It emerged from under the leaves, a nervy thing, one of those phenomenal caranguejeiras the Cocambos call janduçus, a janduçu as big as your hand, Doctor, and about the same color, equally ugly, with the index and ring fingers arched in menace. I hadn't let go of the paddle, which I swung clumsily around in an effort to move the canoe backward or sever the stretch of web linking me to the janduçu, to the gleaming metallic granules such vermin have for eyes, but nothing I did worked: the trembling strands of the silken footbridge led directly to my hair, my mouth. Finally I gained the advantage in this nightmare. The janduçu had fallen: it was gurgling among the igabas and amambis and the purple flowers streaked with slime. Both of us were furiously flailing away—me to break free of the web, the spider to reach the shore or clamber aboard the pirogue.

Synthesize, Golpiez, sighed the psychiatrist. I get it—no need to pile on superfluous details.

I watched the desperate swimmer thash around, growing weaker and weaker. Then it sank.

Neither man spoke for a while. The room was stifling. Each mopped the brackish sweat pearling on his skin.

That's all? asked Gonçalves at last.

Disappointed.

I don't see anything else, replied Fabian.

Contrite.

I'm tired. I'd like the image to persist, but it's fading. Something has come to an end.

Come to an end? You're joking! burst out the psychiatrist. You've got it backwards—everything's just starting! We're only at the beginning! Dig deeper, Golpiez! Go beyond what's fading away!

When Fabian remained silent, Gonçalves stood up. In gesturing, he had struck the mechanical armpiece of the dental chair. The drill bobbed up and down, a toy dangling from a piece of elastic.

We're going to delve into this, Golpiez! I'm not giving up here!

The office had three windows. Two were blocked off by raffia mats. Outside the third, parrots were indulging in squawking contests. The men had to yell to be heard over this frightful din.

Gonçalves drew a curtain over the window on the right, the third one, blotting out the admirable spectacle of everyday life on a street in Puesto Libertad, the wide range of greens after a shower, trees weighed down by aerial roots and local fauna.

Diapotherapy, he announced. We'll continue the investigation from another angle. We'll get back to the beginning in another way.

Whatever you want, Doctor, stammered Fabian.

The office was already dim enough for the slide projector, but Gonçalves fussed briefly over a jammed blind anyway. He stood for a minute before the windows on the left, muttering insanely, banging repeatedly on the mechanism gummed up with gluey pollen, pulling angrily on filthy cords plastered with tiny dead things and cockroaches that had returned to their primeval inexistence. The blind would not budge. Gonçalves abandoned it scornfully.

In any case, he said, if it were too dark you'd fall asleep. I know you, Golpiez! You take every opportunity to escape from the mud of reality into your dreams! I know you inside out!

He set up the slide projector on his desk, among the flower pots and Indian artifacts from the dentist's personal collection. The machine was a small hunk of scrap metal, a piece of military surplus from the time of the rebellion, a magic lantern tiger-striped in khaki and sandy gray to create a camouflage effect. A sturdy model, capable of functioning in times of war and revolution and under all circumstances and absolutely anywhere, even here, in Puesto Libertad, where the electricity had been out for ages. Gonçalves pushed some orchids out of his way, swept aside sacred drums and masato bowls and ornaments of toucan feathers and bracelets of jaguar teeth, rummaged in a drawer to find additional psychotropic implements (a lighter, three handfuls of slides, a blowpipe used to point out this or that significant detail in the image), and, finally, lit the kerosene lamp behind the slide viewer.

The flame flickered, then burned steadily, giving off a yellow light. Fabian stared at the wall, at the empty space between the Cocambo cache-sexes of tapir skin and the decorative shrubs. That was where the glimmering photographs selected by Gonçalves would appear.

This isn't the first time we've worked like this, said the psychiatrist, but let me remind you of the rules. You are to assume that there is no difference between your memory and whatever appears on the wall. You are not allowed to hesitate or remain silent. In principle you may not even attempt to lie. Is that quite clear?

Fabian squinted. He was concentrating. Before him lay one of the winding stretches of the Abacau River, a bend resembling thousands of others with its solid wall of dense foliage, quite lovely, but not very welcoming. In the coves one could make out landslides of red clay, tangles of roots and branches that would have made going ashore difficult indeed. The trees pressed so closely together that they cast no reflection on the gloomy water.

Your vocabulary, Golpiez! exclaimed Gonçalves heatedly. Your language! You're not the only Indian in this room! We're among Jucapiras here. Don't force me to keep saying this! Now, which trees are you talking about?

Muiracutucas, guacuris, jacarandas, mamauranas, iebaros, recited Fabian. On the left, a gnarled cajuçara in full flower. In the first cove, some garapuvu limbs; in the second cove, the dead trunk of an ararani; in the third cove . . .

Okay, said Gonçalves. That's fine.

Outside the office, in the Pasaje 6 de Mayo and farther

away, on the Avenida Bandera, which ran all the way down to the river, the parrots continued to screech in all directions. A band of monkeys replied with equal fervor. One could not have wished for a more appropriate sound track.

The photo was taken a short distance upriver from Puesto Libertad, announced Gonçalves. The person is arriving in a pirogue. You see the prow in the foreground?

That blurry spot?

Gonçalves and his blowpipe did indeed point to the blurry spot. Around the reed mouthpiece of the pipe quivered a strip of dirty fur, from an otter's tail, perhaps, or the breast of a jaratataca, and the strip was attached by a very pretty turquoise clasp.

Yes, there, said Gonçalves. Right in front.

The photo is rather mediocre, observed Fabian.

I couldn't care less about your technical or aesthetic opinions, replied the psychiatrist irritably. I want you to tell me about this arrival in Puesto Libertad. Who is sitting or kneeling in the canoe? Name?

It's a woman, said Fabian uncertainly.

The pirogue was gliding rapidly along the steep river bank, taking advantage of the current; then it slowed and entered a narrow channel that had suddenly appeared amid the seemingly impenetrable foliage. Now it was floating again on that water-plant soup Fabian had mentioned in describing his combat with the giant janduçu.

Gonçalves manipulated the viewer with clangorous haste. He became exasperated when the slide jammed or the flame wavered (disturbed by a draft or a series of murderous diphthongs and fricatives) and shed no light, or when the photograph presented an indecipherable hodgepodge of clayey brown and spinach or pea or bottle or olive or lettuce green, or when the image appeared on the wall upside down and continued to appear thus several times in a row

despite repeated attempts at inversion and reinversion
and despite frantic racking in and out of the slide and
despite curses in Jucapira addressed to the magic lantern,
its inventors, the inventors of photography, the mentally ill
in general, psychiatrists in particular, and the municipal
health department.

Fabian was twisting around in the dental chair, trying to
get a good look at the crooked image. He leaned forward,
stretched, gripped the armrests. Gradually he made out the
Indian woman paddling beneath the overhanging foliage,
alongside a clearing festooned with vines and mosses that
created patches of intense darkness. It was night. Instead of
light and air, there was a mixture of sap, vegetable slimes,
and chlorophyllous froths, as there always is at that hour in
the primeval jungle, in the heart of the rain forest, in the
heart of the flooded caaguaçu: inaccessible, moldering,
impenetrable, suffocating, deadly to the tourist and the
imperialist, incomprehensible to the non-Indian, asphyxiat-
ing to the . . .

No literature, said Gonçalves. It aggravates me when you
break into flourishes. That woman. Her name.

Manda, said Fabian.

You're sure? barked Gonçalves.

The picture's underexposed, explained Fabian. Sure?
Not really. I'm groping in the dark. In any case, she's a
Chikraya. No doubt about that.

No doubt! sputtered the psychiatrist. When Manda is a
Cayacoe name, one hundred percent Cayacoe! Even groping in the dark, this error is unforgivable!

But I thought I'd recognized the Chikraya way of holding
the paddle—with the hand too low on the shaft, insisted
Fabian defensively. And I also thought I'd glimpsed those
typical Chikraya ear ornaments, three black seeds strung on
a stone needle, and there was the Chikraya hairstyle as well,

and her perfume of russet smoke, of smooth bark, of nuts and green papayas, a bouquet that Chikraya women give off when they wish to be seductive or when they feel their final hour is nigh.

I didn't see any earring, muttered Gonçalves to himself.

He was already showing the next slide: a close-up of a stump sticking out of the water. The canoe bumped into it. Fabian described Manda's efforts to get around the obstacle. Manda was unaware that she was babbling a muddle of old revolutionary catchphrases; disoriented by a bout of malaria, she wavered between drowsiness and delirium. She raised the hem of the leafy curtain imprisoning her. She rumpled the garlands of moss, then smoothed them out again. Now she plunged her arm into the foul water, grabbing and shaking spongy, sticky roots she would have found repulsive if she hadn't been half-asleep. An aquatic lizard reared up at her elbow and vanished immediately into the weeds, a tamacuari almost a foot and a half long. The crest on its head glinted with blue reflections, as did its teeth. I'm being influenced here by the deceptive coloring of the slide, obviously.

Doesn't matter, said Gonçalves. Go on. Your relationship with this so-called Chikraya?

My relationship from what angle? asked Fabian.

His voice: tremulous. Fatigue was setting in. He looked up at the shaman-doctor with perplexed and listless eyes.

From the sexual angle, said Gonçalves. You know perfectly well that sexuality is at the core of all our psychological imbalances, Golpiez, much more so than death or the collapse of the revolution. That Chikraya, or rather, that Cayacoe—did you surucate with her?

That may have happened, replied Fabian evasively. Once or twice.

How was it?

Normal.

Uh huh, observed the psychiatrist blandly.

Up on the wall, the slides kept coming. The pace picked up, so that several Indian women paddled in front of Fabian, crossing dead-end channels or stagnant pools at night or in almost complete darkness, appearing one after the other, poorly centered, photographed from the back, in semiprofile from the rear, from too far away. The silence of the forest was dampened by warm and heavy nocturnal dews, by emanations from the lakes, from putrid waters. The canoes advanced slowly toward Puesto Libertad, and in the canoes Indian women murmured old slogans from the time of the guerrilla war, outdated internationalist and egalitarian ideas, and their eyes were closed. They seemed ill, exhausted. Their foreheads and shoulders and chests gleamed wetly. To please Gonçalves, Fabian named them— Manda, Leonor Nieves, María Gabriela—and he admitted having surucated with them, frequently or occasionally. The psychiatrist made grumpy comments under his breath.

Then a man's profile flashed for a moment near the Cocambo cache-sexes of tapir skin.

That one's easy to identify, announced Fabian.

I'm listening, go on.

That's Gutiérrez, he used to be a soldier. He was discharged.

Tell me more about this, ordered Gonçalves, projecting a close-up of the man's head. He was a Coariguaçu with a face pitted by smallpox, and his ugliness had not been improved by fate, hardship, or wounds. A bullet had pierced his upper lip and left cheek, leaving a terrible scar upon his smile, redesigning it with deceitful folds, in artificial puckers and contractures of the kind common only to spies or informers. His slanting eyes reflected the memory of long years of revolutionary struggle, of slinking about, of beatings—

inflicted or endured—by day or night or at any time in between. His eyes also revealed an inclination to bitterness, to sharp-tongued reproaches, and a definite taste for radical solutions, for the violence of anarchism as well as the more disciplined variety practiced by crack army units, vanguard or shock troops.

You're making me dizzy with your pompous exaggerations, complained the psychiatrist. Give us details, Golpiez! Or your audience will lose interest!

This former soldier has just sat down again in the canoe, continued Fabian. He tries to use the paddle, but his right hand shakes too much, and his left arm hangs uselessly, infected with gangrene. He sighs in discouragement, and moans. He's going to faint—he collapses on top of the rotting provisions of fruit . . .

Use their Indian names! Use the vernacular!

He collapses in the rear of the canoe, on the abacaxis, on the various kinds of watermelon, the joromopis, the ibabuçus, the different sorts of mangoes, the apareibas, the overripe guaraparis, the cunapoybas (already bruised, and which he'd do better to throw overboard, since they'll only attract wasps), the pacoinajás, the bananas. Rancid pulp seeps into the crook of his elbow. His left arm slides down toward the water; his hand slips beneath the surface. He has been traveling on the Abacau for days and days, for weeks. He doesn't feel the piranhas tearing at his fingers, he doesn't see that he will soon be drawing alongside the pontoon landing stage at Puesto Libertad, and he's too weak to understand that his journey is coming to an end.

So is our session, announced Gonçalves. We'll continue the day after tomorrow, at the usual time.

The shaman-doctor bent over the projector, cupped his hand around the flame, and blew. In the last photograph, the former soldier's strained, insincere smile faded away.

Then Gutiérrez himself flickered and disappeared, as though absorbed into the wall.

Animals shrieked in the trees of the Pasaje 6 de Mayo. Fabian mopped his cheeks, chin, nape.

To conclude, said Gonçalves, the traditional little procedure. Expel a phrase from your unconscious. No thinking about it, got that? Just let it come straight from your murky depths.

Fabian panted, at the end of his rope, just like the discharged soldier. He listened to the termites grinding away on the framework of the house. He heard monkeys and bats in the treetops outside, behind the raffia mats. Night was falling. The sun had set. Everything panted, waiting for the light to die away.

Out with it! brayed Gonçalves.

My life has been rich in cowardice, exclaimed Fabian.

Good. I've made a note of that. You may go.

Yes, said Fabian.

He was sniffing the way you do when crying, or after sticking your nose into an armful of medicinal flowers with an overpowering scent—guaçatungas, ipecacuanhas—that makes you wonder whether you should pass out or throw up.

2

YOU KNOW, Manda, I said *cowardice*, I said my life had been
rich in cowardice, but for whatever it's worth, it must have
shot up out of my private ooze like a disgusting bubble of
sound, and I had neither the strength nor the presence of
mind to hold it back, but I could have blurted out something else, said for example that my life had been rich in
defeats, in stupid tragedies, rich in failed love affairs, or I
could have presented myself in an even more shameful
light, hinted at something counterrevolutionary behind the
cowardliness, admitted that . . .

Really, Fabianito, are you rehearsing for your next session
with Gonçalves? asked Manda.

She had her Saturday-afternoon voice, frayed and hoarse
from a week's toil in the local vegetable-oil mill.

In the hut on the Calle Escalante, they were both
stretched out on Manda's bed, listening to the uproar created high in the trees by those tiny monkeys the imperialists
call marmosets, which squabble constantly, chasing one
another from vine to vine, reveling in shrill insults.

It had rained. Victims of the intertribal conflict began landing in puddles—first the floppy caterpillars that had served as projectiles, but then the combatants themselves, saguipiranga marmosets, tamarins, cuxiús with their snarling little carnivorous maws, baby saguijubas and other peevish dwarfs. I wasn't short of names. Among the papers the dentist had abandoned before his execution were the notes for a dictionary of the common native language. The list of monkeys was several pages long. I'd read it, learned it by heart.

You understand, my little Chikraya? murmured Fabian.

Their two bodies at the center of the oppressive heat: prostrate, and sweating buckets. The temperature had dropped barely one degree during the shower, and now it was going up again.

The monkeys had crossed the Calle Escalante and were working their way through people's gardens down to the shantytown called Manuela Aratuípe. It was easier to talk now. Manda sat up on one elbow. She hadn't answered Fabian. She was intrigued by a scratchy clicking noise near her head. Something velvety recoiled into the shadows. A nhanduguaca was creeping around between the pillow and the wall. Manda swatted it expertly, sending it flying across the room after a murderous scraping against the wallboards. The spider landed to the right of the door, beneath the oil stove, with a soft, crumpling thud. Manda and Fabian relaxed again. The nhanduguaca contracted in little jerks, pretending to be comatose, or perhaps it was sincere, slipping regretfully into that last unconscious darkness.

Fabianito, said Manda.

Along the Calle Escalante wafted the first wisps of smoke from charcoal fires, the first warm smells of cooking oil. Earthenware dishes clattered in a nearby hut. The threadbare peace settling over the neighborhood was punctuated by scattered echoes of conversation from the street or the kitchen gardens on either side of it.

The evening would bring no relief from the heat.

Fabianito, my madman, said Manda.

She was whispering, her lips close to Fabian's ear, as though—despite the late hour and the weekend—a spy from the security forces had been crouching on the other side of the wall, listening to their secrets in order to repeat them all down at headquarters on the Calle 19 de Febrero. You could imagine some anonymous informer, or even give a name and face to that man hidden in the weeds—call him Rui Gutiérrez, the former soldier, snooping and ferreting about out of jealousy, sheer spite, or the desire to remain faithful to the idea of the revolutionary police . . . or the even cruder and less nostalgic idea of the police, plain and simple.

You know I'm not a Chikraya, said Manda. You're confusing me with someone else, with Leonor Nieves. Me, I'm a Cayacoe. Come on, we've known each other for thirty years. You could correct yourself when you make a mistake, you know.

He moved restlessly next to her in the twilight. The memory of Leonor Nieves always upset him. Eager to change the subject, he complained about the torrid humidity, the mosquitoes; he wriggled around trying to get comfortable, fussing like a sleepless old Indian, with great hacking and throat clearing. Deploring the poor state of the straw mattress, he rolled over and stretched out again on his side. The coconut fibers sticking up from the bedsprings pierced right through the thin straw pallet, poking him in the back and buttocks. Finally he placed his hand on Manda's belly, just below her navel. Her skin was soaking wet. He explored lower, to the right, the left; she was all sticky, proof of the friendly generosity with which they'd just romped and coupled.

I like surucating with you, he said, hoping to banish the specter of Leonor Nieves that had come between them.

But now Manda was restless.

Fabianito, she said, I'm worried by these confusions growing inside that cranium of yours. You should stop the sessions with Gonçalves. I think they're hurting you.

Yes, he sighed. But if I stop, the trouble will start again. The inquiry.

For a minute their thoughts ran in the same direction, followed precisely the same path, beginning with Fabian's arrival in Puesto Libertad at the end of June and continuing all through July and August, a nasty time for Fabian. The men in that place on the Calle 19 de Febrero had interrogated him closely and methodically, with particular interest in the misdeeds of his militant life. Day after day he had regurgitated before them the little he knew about Pomponi's assassination, about the disappearance of Judge Pomponi, and he'd vomited bits and pieces of his own youth, his years at the front, in this or that surgical unit or ambulance corps, and then the years spent in Mapiaupi, in one or another department of the hospital, during the crucial great offensives. A very bad time. Since the interrogators were Auguanis, they were not inclined to be lenient or sympathetic to their Jucapira suspect. Fabian found himself at their mercy. He had no legal status. Without a favorable decision from the Calle 19 de Febrero, the local council would not issue him a residence permit. Manda had advised Fabian to register at the municipal health department as a mentally ill person. She knew the psychiatrist, the only shaman-doctor in Puesto Libertad, who wouldn't think twice about discovering serious psychic damage in his future patient. Fabian's inscription on the list of mental defectives had posed no problem and brought several advantages, in particular the payment of an invalid's pension (a pittance, of course), and above all the immediate closure of his file at the Calle 19 de Febrero. On the other hand, Fabian had had to submit to the treatment devised by Gonçalves, which was painful, exhausting, and endless.

Ask for an appointment with the authorities, with the committee, whispered Manda. Perhaps María Gabriela will deign to see you. You'll explain your situation to her. She was once attracted to you. Perhaps she'll help you.

Useless, she's too important. She's forgotten me. She won't help me.

Try anyway.

Useless, repeated Fabian stubbornly.

They lay motionless for a moment, hand in hand, two strays deeply attached to one another, rotting away between downpours in Puesto Libertad, surrounded by the bickering of hairy marmosets and then enveloped in the evening silence, inside a dilapidated hut, on a straw mattress smelling of sleep and sex and Saturday-afternoon sexual misery, while over by the oil stove lay the blackish mass of the spider, probably deceased.

Someone crouching behind the shack stretched his limbs, preparing to steal away, and snapped some twigs despite all his precautions. He was going to crawl through the weeds of the garden, slip through the bamboo grove to the Calle Escalante, proceed to the Calle Comandantes, then head up the Avenida Bandera, turn right onto the Calle 19 de Febrero, and there, before Judge Pomponi's assessor, or before some even more narrow-minded and niggling Auguani underling, make his report.

Fabian swallowed hard. Manda heard him gulp, divined his growing anxiety, and tried to distract and reassure him.

Me, too, Fabianito. I like surucating with you, too.

3

JULY, AUGUST.
Recollection.
That less-than-shining summer.
Judge Pomponi's assessor had summoned me for the day. I arrived in the morning at the headquarters of the political security unit, on the Calle 19 de Febrero, where the assessor interviewed me briefly. He reminded me that my dossier lacked some important documents. The investigators had not been pleased with my answers to their questions. Some aspects of my biography required further elucidation: my relations with a few members of the Bandera, my relations with the guerillas of Yaguatinga, with the insurrectionary groups in Mapiaupi, with María Gabriela, with Leonor Nieves, with Pomponi, and the circumstances surrounding my so-called heroic death in Mapiaupi, down by the river in the Cocambo section of town. The investigators had not been able to obtain reliable information on all those points. Consequently, concluded the judge's assessor, my position in Puesto Libertad remained very, very precarious.

Then the door of the office closed behind me and I was handed over to some Auguanis, who were either bare-chested or wearing filthy undershirts or short-sleeved military shirts reeking of sweat and blood. They led me down a dim corridor and ordered me to wait, to hunker down on the floor and not move—and wait.

I tried to doze in the deserted corridor, to stop thinking for an hour or two. Then other Auguanis—half-naked or with their uniform shirts unbuttoned—came to fetch me for the next stage of the interrogation, which sometimes took place in one of the ground-floor offices but more often occurred outside, unseen from the street but in full view of the green waves of forest that began right behind the building. Depending on the day and the various specialities of my inquisitors, I was treated to screams of abuse in Auguani slang, icily furious tirades in the common native language, or threats with a machete, or mock executions against the palisade, in either of the two courtyards. The second one, the kitchen yard, was the largest. We went through our paces in the pouring rain or the broiling sunshine, obliged to yell louder than the downpour thundering into the mud or the perpetual chirring of the cicadas or the chattering of the parrots and monkeys. In the kitchen yard, where they kept meat safes and fish tanks, they forced me to watch the cooks cut the throats of their victims and hack them apart. They gutted monkeys, snakes, tortoises, and sometimes the creatures imperialists call crocodiles and we call jacarés—yes, sometimes even giant jacarés.

Whenever they questioned me about my identity, my true nature, some Auguani would always insist that I wasn't a pure-blooded Indian. The implication was that although the Jucapiras should be in a separate class, like the Cocambos, they do not possess the harmless character of the Cocambos, who do not believe in the reality of the world;

thus the Jucapiras come and go insidiously among the Indians even though they are less Indian than the rest. They tested my vocabulary, pointing out trees growing on the other side of the palisade, beyond the jacaré pond, and challenging me to give their Auguani names quickly and correctly, but no matter how well I performed, one or two Auguanis would always say that a Jucapira's nasal sounds are like imperialist diphthongs, that the Jucapiras draw out silent syllables like imperialists, like tourists. Then I'd have to explain certain episodes of my love life or my revolutionary days. Together we'd reopen old chapters and old wounds.

I was a regular in the kitchen yard. How well I came to know the palisade that traced an impassable, tortuous line around its perimeter. They'd sit me down with my back against the bamboo stakes, facing the July or August sun, while one of the cooks in charge of my dossier would verify the keenness of his machete on the Auguani viands, on the victuals that trembled between life and death.

I have only to close my eyes to see that enclosure again: the meat blocks encrusted with blood, the flies, the tub of chicken feet and heads turning blue, left to rot before being dumped into the jacaré pond, practically straight into the crocodiles' jaws.

On the left, the grayish posts behind which the tortoises are penned.

On the right, the pickets to which they attach the monkeys to decapitate and skin them.

And everywhere, the smells of bloody meat or of meat-in-waiting, musing philosophically in the cages or out in the fetid muck.

The investigators compelled me to watch scenes of martyrdom, of dismemberment, and then would slowly draw their greasy blades along my collarbones, from one side to the other, in an effort to learn something more of my connections with Leonor Nieves or María Gabriela or Judge Pomponi before his assassination.

I denied ever having met Leonor Nieves, thus avoiding having to reveal whether or not I'd surucated with her, and I stood firm whenever they questioned the sincerity of my affection for Judge Pomponi and the revolutionary principles for which he fought, but waves of nausea would often sweep away the answers those Auguani brutes were waiting to hear.

I vomited a lot. I knew they wouldn't keep me overnight, preferring to summon me again the next day or the one after that. I knew they'd send me home — but not without immediately spreading the rumor that I'd spilled my guts denouncing my former comrades in the civil war. The afternoon was growing mild. I buried my vomit under a few handfuls of dust, stood up, and leaned against the palisade. My retching hadn't made the authorities of the Calle 19 de Febrero more favorably disposed toward me. The interrogation began again.

I caught my breath and looked up at the sky. More gray showed through the gaps in the foliage, and from time to time I spotted large bats whirling around the treetops, their impressive wings already unfurled a bit ahead of schedule. I thought about the peace and quiet that would soon arrive, and prepared myself for twilight. Mentally I ran down the list of trees that overhung the courtyard. I felt so overcome with emotion that I had to prove to myself that my true nature was Indian, that the Jucapiras were Indians and knew the common tongue. I looked at the majestic trees and I named them: timbauvas, atiribas, muchurís, jipis, biratingas, matambus, iauacanos, jaraguamurus, sucuúbas, sucuubaranas.

4

IN OCTOBER, I said.

In October, the rains came. Cloudbursts poured down endlessly on Puesto Libertad and the surrounding virgin forest. Lagoons and marshes overflowed. The Abacau rose and tore away its banks in vast gulps, swallowing whatever was worm-eaten or poorly fastened or plain unlucky in the riverside district. During the summer I'd watched temporary constructions appear along the Embarcadero Fusilados del 31 de Agosto, among the peninsulas of reeds and the landing stages of the shipyard, but now there was a radical cleanup going on in the easily flooded sections of the lower part of town. Anything temporary was being wiped out.

For example, I said.

Suddenly, for example, a shanty would tip out over the swirling water and break apart, exposing to wind and waves its hastily cobbled-together construction, along with a hammock swinging between two nails, and inside the hammock, as though already wrapped in a shroud of netting, a

Cocambo long ready for the voyage, or an Indian woman whom illness and decrepitude had . . .

Enough, Golpiez! I told myself loudly.

Rudely interrupting my own story. I'd felt it necessary to introduce Gonçalves's voice here, with its easily imitable exasperation.

Enough of that cheap sentimentality for suckers. You've made your point—no need to belabor it. Talk, don't snivel. Talk about the rain.

Fine, I said. These discreet disintegrations were lost amid the crackling din; you couldn't hear a thing anymore but the noise of the storm. My head rumbled constantly with thunder and flashed with lightning. Before Indian eyes stagnated glimmers of sea-green bronze. I could hear the moaning of the pilings down by the river, the grating of logs, dugout canoes, the corpses of Cocambos wedged under the wharf by the river.

Ah! I said. So despite the uproar, you could hear things after all! Another contradiction in your story, Golpiez!

It was quite close, a hundred yards away, I argued. The boards creaked.

Come on, Golpiez, tell us instead where you were living. Reliable and verifiable information. Cough up the address. Without disguising anything—spit it out right now.

Of course, Doctor, I sighed.

I was living on the Calle 30 de Abril, amid the ruins of a shantytown reclaimed by creeping plants. A ten-minute walk through the snake-infested brush took me to the Avenida Bandera and civilization. I would have liked to live on the Calle Escalante, in one of the empty huts slowly falling to pieces around Manda's garden, but the central residential districts were closely controlled by the local council and were thus off-limits to people like me, saddled with a suspicious past, an open file with the political security forces, and a present that was very, very precarious.

Cozy is not a word that springs to mind to describe my home. I'd built and furnished it from odds and ends, without enthusiasm. Partitions of woven palm leaves, old matting and old wall paneling and old frame pieces dug out of piles of debris; the door stolen from the Calle Escalante, pilfered at night, with the help of Rui Gutiérrez; some pots contributed by my Cocambo or Jabaana neighbors, a basin from Manda, a lamp found in the slum settlement of Manuela Aratuípe; a hammock.

All right, Golpiez. And the glimmers of sea-green bronze. We've got the picture on the decor. Now, the main characters. Your Manda, your Gutiérrez. Then the others.

Yes, I said.

Time passed. I lived with no thought of tomorrow. Manda worked in the municipal oil mill as a packer. She would smuggle out the waste grease for us, inferior by-products that wound up in Gutiérrez's hut and mine, where they burned either rapidly or very poorly, with great hissing and stinking smoke. Still, this way we saved a few dollars.

Dollars! I exclaimed. In the rain forest! That vile word! What a shameful lapse, Golpiez! I insist on an Indian word. Not that imperialist term!

A few abanis, I said, amending my account with a word no one used. We saved a few abanis. A handful. Every bit helps.

I was no longer always hanging about at Manda's the way I had in July and August, and in any case she'd given me a day for my visits. Rui Gutiérrez had his day, too: Sunday. I'd spend a good part of Saturday with Manda, reminiscing in a hushed voice about old times, listening to the breathing of Gutiérrez or other informers behind the wall.

Did you surucate?

Yes.

How was it?

The way it is when you're fifty: no rapture, no illusions, remembering the voluptuous giddiness of the years when the revolution was still alive.

Good. Continue.

I began spending more time with Rui Gutiérrez, the former soldier. He would come knocking at my door a little before midday. We had a tacit understanding. I tried to stifle my suspicions about him, suspicions aroused by something of the policeman in his way of speaking and his silences. I forced myself not to believe that he would go repeat our conversations in that place on the Calle 19 de Febrero. As for him, he made an effort to overlook the fact that I hadn't won glory and an internationalist revolutionary medal, as he had. He leaned toward the idea that I'd never hold out against the Auguanis of the Calle 19 de Febrero, that I'd cave in and denounce anybody who came to mind, and that I claimed to be a revolutionary more from necessity than conviction. He wasn't constantly throwing that in my face, though.

Gutiérrez's savage bitterness.

The disappointment that ate away at him when he compared Puesto Libertad with what he had fought for.

What he had died for.

The way he turned his disappointment into sarcasm or unfairness.

The way he sought out intoxicating pleasures as sordid as those of the Cocambos in the town slums.

Manda would defend him to me. He had some trouble with the military authorities, she said. The same problem as you've got with that investigation down at the Calle 19 de Febrero. Put yourself in his place, Fabianito. An exemplary internationalist career, participation in several decisive campaigns, a hero's death, not like ours at Mapiaupi, almost accidental, incidental—no, a death in the company of those shot on the thirty-first of August—and then he winds up in Puesto Libertad in the shantytown of Manuela Aratuípe, with a measly pension and the cold shoulder from the Department of Military Affairs, and no support from anyone but those idiots in political security. That's what has embittered him, poor Rui. He expected better treatment. Don't be impatient with him, Fabianito.

Gutiérrez would turn up at my door, having drained a gourd of manioc wine along the way; often he'd have stopped down by the docks to drink a cup of that fermented sap and saliva concoction brewed by the Cocambo locals, and, staggering a bit, he'd pour out his grievances about his army discharge, or he'd grin that disturbing smile of his and try to provoke me into saying something bad about the authorities or María Gabriela or the Bandera or the political security forces, something I'd never allowed myself to do in his presence.

You see, Golpiez, he'd mumble, shaking his head so befuddled by war and decisive campaigns and alcohol. You see, we had a right to think that Puesto Libertad would be the final stage.

It will never get better, I'd say.

Our dialogue after that.

We're not going to get bogged down here, Golpiez. We've still got a long way to go.

To go where?

Trust me.

You've got a plan?

Trust me, I tell you.

And that air of his, the air of a drunken conspirator, an air that could inspire a wide range of very definite feelings, none of which had anything to do with trust.

5

WE'RE GOING to get out of here. I've got a plan.

The clinic? Shamanism?

My voice: flat, listless. We'd already had this conversation the day before and the day before that and throughout the whole month of October. Same words, same tone.

Yes, exclaimed Gutiérrez, just getting warmed up. We'll go up the Abacau, Golpiez. We'll press on beyond the headwaters if we must.

Beyond the marshes?

But it was just to humor him, keep him talking. I knew the itinerary by heart.

Farther, farther. We're going to find a spot for guys like us. We'll set up a clinic, and we'll use that as our base to found a utopian territory. There'll be only Jabaanas, Cocambos, and us.

And the permits, the visa from the authorities?

They can go fuck themselves, he said gloomily.

So we requisition the canoes, head upriver, get beyond the lake, the marshes. Then what?

Then we make ourselves at home deep in the rain forest, Golpiez. We open up a shaman's dispensary and start to live the good life. We'll have an easy-going clientele, not particular about our methods, indifferent to whatever our pasts might offer of shame or glory.

I objected. Revolutionary morale, technical problems, hygiene, relations with the masses, relations with the Jabaanas (who display an even greater reluctance to survive than the Cocambos do), the poor quality of the care we'd be claiming to offer . . .

Listen, it's not like that at all, he assured me. Nothing's stopping us. Anyone at all can restore ailing souls, it's an internationalist duty like any other. You were a medical orderly; you could make sure that we don't make any serious mistakes. And we've had some experience—don't forget your treatment with Gonçalves. We'll be relieving the Indians' pain, Golpiez. It'll be our turn to play shaman-doctors. We can't be worse than Gonçalves.

Leave him out of this, I said. He hasn't done anything to you.

We'll organize a utopian territory, said Gutiérrez after a moment of silence. Far from heroes.

At last, I said.

Can't you just imagine? he asked eagerly.

I barely replied. I could just imagine.

6

AND MARÍA Gabriela? asked Gutiérrez suddenly.

I pretended I hadn't heard clearly because of the spitting and crackling of the fire.

She's the big boss in this town, he continued. That place on the Calle 19 de Febrero does whatever she says. I don't know why you won't insist on seeing her. After all, you had an affair with her, didn't you?

There was suddenly something policemanlike in the way Gutiérrez was sticking out his jaw. He was trying to pump me. I wasn't answering. I leaned over the fire again and stirred up the flames. We were roasting two and a half yards of water snake. In front of witnesses, I would probably have wondered out loud about exactly what kind we were grilling: a golden ibinayaya or a jabotiboia or a muçurana or a caçabóia. But in my interior monologues, I'm not so picky about my vocabulary.

So many years have passed, I observed.

You think she's forgotten you?

More than likely, I sighed. I must occupy a pretty insignificant place in her memory, right up there with invertebrates and nameless things that live in mud flats.

Neither of us spoke for a minute. We turned over the golden ibinayaya, which seemed in danger of charring. The grease was smoking.

Fat chance, said Gutiérrez.

What do you mean?

The members of the Bandera never forget, replied Gutiérrez. Not even in death.

7

YOU DON'T want to talk about Yaguatinga yet, Golpiez? About Mapiaupi? That night in Yaguatinga?

No, not yet, I said.

You don't feel ready?

No. It'll have to wait.

All right, then establish that autumnal ambience once again, Golpiez. October, early November in Puesto Libertad. That not intranquil period of your life.

Relatively not intranquil, I remarked.

On days when it rained heavily, I didn't get any visitors. I daydreamed, drowsing in my hammock for hours, all functions at half-speed, my belly empty. Wrapped in shadows, I studied the ants, their marching and countermarching. The list of ants is extensive. Gonçalves often used to read me extracts from it to hypnotize me. He read from those notes for a dictionary of the common native language that the dentist had left behind in his desk when he went off to the Calle 19 de Febrero. I reviewed all the names I could remember, almost as many as those for the trees.

Don't go into all that now, Golpiez, I scolded myself. Save the list for later. The imperialist word is okay for just setting the stage.

Calamities befell the ants, I continued. To the left, the streaming rain; to the right, a chameleon lying in wait. Formic life isn't a bowl of cherries, either. I didn't envy them.

Next, the spiders.

Avoiding the chameleon, they'd crawl heavily from their hiding places to look for drier digs.

I watched them sidle along the palm branches, at the edge of the roof.

Extricating myself from the hammock, I picked up a machete and went after their nests.

The spiders faced this threat coolly. When they felt targeted by the trajectory of my blade, they dashed for the dark tunnels between the boards or fell to the sodden ground and lay still, cleverly pretending to have been squashed by my attack. Or they reared up and trotted boldly to meet me.

Massive, powerful creatures.

I hacked away with heated, steamy savagery. Everything was hissing—the reed partitions, the scampering tarantulas, the planks laid over the mud, my feet slipping on the . . .

The tarantulas were hissing too? I asked, seized with sudden misgivings.

You hear something when they rush at you, I explained. A kind of hairy mumbling.

Watch out what you try to put over, Golpiez, I advised. Certain plot twists are permissible, others not.

You do hear something, I insisted. The nightmare instinct in us perceives vibrations and interprets them as noise.

Barely passable, I said. You'd better wind it up.

The twisted hammock swung back and forth behind me; the shadows teemed with activity; raindrops filtering through the roof splashed onto my bare legs, my torn undershirt, my sweaty forehead, my hands. Lightning struck Puesto Libertad again and again. The whole world was an infernal drum.

That, according to Gutiérrez, was what we should leave behind by going up the river to its source and beyond, to the lakes where the great anacondas sleep, and farther on, to regions inhabited by no one, not even heroes.

8

THE PSYCHIATRIST'S office, formerly the dentist's.

New plants had taken root at the base of the walls. They climbed, branched out, and smelled like a jacaré pond.

That fetid odor, so unappetizing.

A lizard skittered along a vine, then out the window on the right. It had been frightened by the shamanistic exclamations of Gonçalves.

I don't remember anymore, repeated Fabian. I swear to you, Doctor. My memories just stop. There's nothing there.

Scrounge around, Golpiez! Break through that resistance! shouted the psychiatrist.

The mechanical armpiece squeaked and jiggled over Fabian's head. Whenever the dangling drill stopped bouncing, Gonçalves would send the armpiece a right jab, followed by a left hook to the rubber tubing.

Drill holes in your memory, dig down to the pulp! Never mind the pain, Golpiez, excavate! Gouge deeply! Wreak havoc if that's what it takes!

His bellowing echoed from branch to branch; then

everything lay low for about ten seconds, quivering only with extreme prudence and in retreat or more softly than a whisper. The sole creature to make itself conspicuous was a millipede that had wandered into the optical system of the projector, and its monstrous silhouette writhed in agony on the wall.

Silence. Deep silence.

Fabian's eyelids fluttered. He couldn't manage to focus on Gonçalves's wrinkled face, so representative of the ghastly mask that settles over the features of Jucapiras as they approach old age or death. Fabian lowered his gaze. Beneath the white smock Gonçalves slipped on before these sessions to protect himself from dream splinters, his emaciated, almost nude body was panting. When the smock yawned open, Fabian had the impression that he was contemplating his own carcass struggling against asphyxiation. He noticed the caramel-colored spots, the gray scars, everything that had been engraved there during the years of fighting and the years of forgetting, everything that told a tale of slow disintegration in the heart of the flooded rain forest, the crossing of venomous regions, unfortunate encounters, interrogations out under the trees, sickness, death, sudden outbreaks of rebellion in the villages, endless internationalist campaigns.

Let's start again, snarled Gonçalves. A train station, you were saying. The station at Yaguatinga. I doubt that there was ever a railroad line in that area, but we'll let that pass. The main thing is that you've begun to talk. For the moment, that's the essential thing. You mentioned a building across from the station.

A hotel, said Fabian. A run-down hotel.

What the hell were you up to in Yaguatinga, Golpiez? Sent there on a mission by the Bandera?

He no longer reminded Fabian to look at the slide,

because the superimposition of the now expired millipede made the image indecipherable.

He'd started braying and shaking the armrest of the dental chair again.

I never belonged to the Bandera, said Fabian.

Well then, why were you loafing around Yaguatinga? Tourism?

I was returning from the front, explained Fabian. I'd been serving as a medical orderly.

Which front? roared Gonçalves. At Yaquacre?

I don't know anymore, said Fabian.

An orderly with the government troops or with the revolutionary forces? screeched Gonçalves.

Impossible for me to remember, Doctor, whimpered Fabian. Despite my assiduous digging, I haven't turned up that information. The hole in my memory remains empty.

Gonçalves shrugged, then turned to clean the glass plate of the slide viewer, the magic lantern besmirched by a thousand scorched little legs.

The image was crisp again: a dusty town square surrounded by low, nondescript houses, with a few Indians sitting or crouching or lounging or lying dead against the walls.

Yaguatinga, said Gonçalves. I'm listening. And it's in your interest to come up with something solid for me, if you don't want me to denounce you to the health department as a faker.

You'd do that? asked Fabian, wincing.

You bet, said Gonçalves.

9

ALSO, IF you could vary your rhythm—there's something about your manner of speaking that gets my back up. That inconclusive, nagging tone you use to describe your squalid life.

And speak up, damn it! As if you had no idea that my hearing . . . my ears . . . You know all about that disastrous operation . . . And to top it off, the constant, strident whirring of the insects, as though the rain forest were one big madhouse . . . All that chitin vibrating more wildly than a drill . . .

The hotel across from the train station in Yaguatinga looked like a farm built out of cinder blocks or, rather, like an oversized pigsty. The masons had walked off the job several years earlier, leaving the unfinished hotel to grow older and older without a hope of ever being free of gray cement rubble and blotches of plaster. A door with broken windows stood half-open in the middle of the facade, as though permanently obstructed by the unevenness of the rough terrain. Above it sat an abortive attempt at a second story, where scattered stubs of bricks and lumber betrayed the abandoned beginnings of a wall. The original project had evolved, and in some places there were the rough outlines of a terrace, or a tile roof slanting toward an interior courtyard. There was nothing inviting about this square edifice, which sported a single door and a few barred dormer windows. I contemplated without enthusiasm the rusty spikes pointing heavenward, the vestiges of some misguided framework.

It was late in the day; the sky seemed leaden.

I'd set my shapeless soldier's pack down in front of me on the dirt road, still undecided about the best way to spend the night in Yaguatinga. I pondered the problem.

The country bus on which I'd spent three bone-rattling days had just left. I stood there with my back to the station. The dust was settling, an irritating dust full of the ugliness of such places. Indians had already staked their claims to the open-air dormitory at the foot of the station's facade, each one peevishly marking off his personal territory with fruit peels and other garbage or with scraps of rag, using gobs of spittle to complete a perimeter it was unwise to cross without permission. There were Coariguaçus, Sobiberots, Yasseguaras.

I considered finding a spot elsewhere, at the entrance to a small street or somewhere near the tracks, but in an unfamiliar town, people are reluctant to make their nests far from a group. Vagabonds always have their reasons for gathering in a particular place. Some reasons are obvious— access to a water faucet, for example—while others are more mysterious, rooted in our ancestral animal heritage. The attraction of crowding together, of sharing one's filth and fear.

Spare us your sociological blather, Golpiez, said Gonçalves. But continue, continue.

Fabian studied the railroad tracks that sliced through Yaguatinga on cement ties laid over the hard ground, beaten earth stained with dirty oil. The tracks followed the main road. The homes along this grimy street seemed deserted; no lights of any kind, no flames from lamp or stove flickered in the mud-walled houses and shacks. At the end of the street, the tracks slipped on out of town, past the sheds at the depot and the military post, then stopped just beyond a dump—or perhaps continued on in an abandoned line, through clumps of large, prickly leaves, toward stony wastes, toward stretches of red and ochre and brown gravel, then ventured still farther, plunged inside old mining concessions, crossing wilderness, rebel-controlled territories, and unexplorable zones designated on government maps by dotted lines, hatchings, or blanks.

Electric lights blinked on atop a few poles, calling attention to the darkness of the night now gathering on the roofs and promising to pour down very soon into the streets.

These roofs of zinc or tarred thatch were fast growing indistinguishable against the dark green of the surrounding hills.

Hold it, Golpiez! shouted Gonçalves. Stop right there! The hills around Yaguatinga are quite rocky. The landscape is green, true, but not so green as that. The forest out there isn't dense at all. Your color scheme is all wrong.

I shrugged. The objection was meaningless. Nightfall had already swamped the spectrum, which was fading away into shades that were all pretty much alike.

Well, go on, Golpiez.

A militiaman stood next to the station, as though to ensure an orderly sunset. This unarmed, affable militiaman was the sole visible representative of the government's forces. One might have thought he'd parked himself in front of the bullet-scarred wall and grubby ticket window

with specific orders to await the inevitable burst of machine-
gun fire from a guerrilla fighter lurking up an alley, in an
anonymous window, or on a corner of the Plaza Central.

Fabian picked up his pack by the strap and walked away
from the militiaman and the Coariguaçu or Yasseguara
derelicts and their spit-gob frontiers. He wanted to wash his
face after his long bus trip. He headed for the hotel.

The hotel lobby was an unfurnished area, a mere exten-
sion of the corridor, originally intended to welcome guests
but now serving to preserve the odors left behind over the
years by transient Indians (the reek of worn-out shoes,
worn-out and moth-eaten clothing, worn-out and moth-
eaten and broken-down bodies), smells to which were
added hints of chicken droppings and rabbit litter drifting
in from the courtyard. Fabian counted three doors on each
side of the hall. He supposed they led to a series of rooms. At
the far end, the seventh door was ajar, allowing Fabian to
glimpse a hint of twilight and a patch of grass. When he had
pulled the door panel toward him and stepped over the
plank that formed a kind of absurd doorstop across the
threshold, he found himself in a patio with a chicken coop,
a rabbit hutch, toilets, a sink, and a clothesline on which
hung a blue towel. Behind the line were a gallery and two
or three rooms that resembled cells, for although they
were without doors, their skylights were furnished with
sinister-looking bars. On the opposite side, a second, identical gallery . . .

That'll do, Golpiez! You're cluttering up the picture with
your details. Get to the point!

Fabian went over to the recess containing the latrines and
the sink to wash himself. The light was dying. No one from
the hotel had appeared. Fabian put his shirt back on,
rebuckled his knapsack, and left the courtyard. He made
noise in the corridor, hoping to attract the attention of the

Indian man or woman who rented out the rooms or the beds or, at least, the corners where you could lie down and sleep. In the lobby, a light bulb of feeble wattage at the end of a wire that . . .

Stop! You're wasting time in descriptions that lead nowhere! Didn't you promise to talk about some Indian woman?

I'm getting there, said Fabian.

I'm still waiting, said Gonçalves.

Fabian proceeded down the hall, stomping loudly, and he had just halted beneath the bare bulb when one of the doors opened. He whirled, almost bumping into a Chikraya woman in her prime, about twenty-seven or twenty-eight years old. She was smiling. The Indian had the lovely face of a resistance fighter, with delicate features and dark, dark eyes in whose depths one could read the traces of an already turbulent past, one torn by wrenching farewells and violence, yet still unstained by baseness. Tossing her head, this woman—who clearly harbored dreams of ruthless victory—shook out her unbraided but clean and neatly combed hair, and Fabian breathed in the scent that clung to her, a blend of fleeting, enchanting effects like the shimmer of shot silk; smoke glowing red at sunset; a sandy river bank at the first caress of dawn; the polished surface of a lake, of the lake where the serpent sleeps, that Mother-of-all-waters; the forest at night; gray dewdrops. Then Fabian smelled her warm brown skin.

The Chikraya looked Fabian up and down with amusement. There was an air of availability about her of which she was perhaps unaware, a willful independence that excited attention and curiosity. She seemed to take Fabian for the manager or a hotel employee. When she touched one ear, Fabian noticed an ornament commonly worn by young Chikraya women: three hard, round seeds threaded onto a stone needle.

My lantern has gone out, she said. The reservoir is empty. Could you . . .

She realized she was face to face with a stranger, an unknown Jucapira of about her own age, but that didn't bother her.

Fabian at the time: typical Jucapira features, immediately recognizable. And everyone knows that women find Jucapiras attractive, at least before old age and their distress over bungling their lives and their regret at having misunderstood their own history transform the Jucapira face into a withered and even hideous caricature.

Keep your insulting comments to yourself, Golpiez.

I wasn't thinking of you, Doctor. I was speaking in general terms.

Well of course, said Gonçalves acidly. You're not talking about me. You have no idea that I'm personally overwhelmed by old age and distraught at having made a botch of my life.

Come now, said Fabian.

In any case, you'll end up like me, growled Gonçalves. When the time comes to return to that primeval inexistence, all Jucapiras are the same. But let's get on with it. The Indian woman, Fabian. Night had fallen over Yaguatinga.

Fabian, as I was saying, had always been popular with Indians, the girls of easy virtue and the whores or semi-prostitutes he sought out when he wasn't busy defending the revolution with the government troops or the rebel forces. But this one, this Chikraya, was definitely first-class. Fabian's heart began to race recklessly. He sensed that the body of this Chikraya—so close to him—welcomed this intimate interest, and even returned it. Something had passed between them, binding them in a conversation without words.

What a load of crap, grumbled Gonçalves.

The Chikraya had realized that Fabian was not a hotel employee and she was about to laugh at her mistake when the bulb in the fixture overhead went out. At the same instant, all light filtering in from the street through the broken windows in the front door simply vanished.

The entire town was in darkness. Fabian remembered the militiaman in front of the train station and imagined him shrinking into the center of all that coal-black space, waiting for the moment when his execution would begin and he could relax. There would be a burst of machine-gun fire, and bullets would cut him down. Then he'd be able to collapse without fear among the indifferent beggars. He'd lie there, like a stupefied Cocambo, as though he were searching peacefully for a way to avoid dying ever again.

Fabian thought of the Chikraya breathing there beside him. She hadn't drawn back—on the contrary. Within a few seconds, a rumbling thundered over Yaguatinga, then died away. The guerrillas had just blown up a pylon or a power relay station.

The darkness intensified the odor around Fabian, the odor of gray dewdrops and sandy river banks and forests just before dawn and the lake haunted by the serpent that is the Mother-of-all-waters.

The Chikraya stirred. The guerrillas have blown up the power station, she said.

Fabian reached out toward her. He felt her arm, her shoulder, her hair; he drew softly closer to the earring, touching the black beads that were the same temperature as the flesh they adorned, those grains of yacaratia or jarinú— I can't remember, the name escapes me—and then he spoke, too.

Yes, the guerrillas must have blown up the power station.

10

STRANGE PLACE, that deserted hotel, remarked the shaman-doctor. But continue, Golpiez.

He didn't sleep that night, said Fabian. Then he did fall asleep, but he woke up with a start because of a nightmare.

The Chikraya was stretched out next to him on the bed, which had no sheets, only grime-stiffened blankets, starched by the leavings of previous travelers. She was lying in a lover's position, her left thigh and hip leaning against him, but she was awake now, and soon she rolled onto her side, placing her hand limply between Fabian's legs. He sensed, however, that she was no longer playing with him and that she was on the alert, listening to the rattle of automatic weapons in the distance. She was trying to understand what was happening on the outskirts of Yaguatinga. She propped herself up on one elbow to hear better. As she breathed, one nipple would brush against Fabian's arm and withdraw, touch him lightly, and withdraw.

Fabian felt as though he'd always loved this woman to distraction, as though he'd shared hundreds and hundreds of nights of delirious complicity with her.

Now they were both listening.

Automatic-weapons fire rattled off in the distance. Just outside the town, the insurgents may have been wasting time in ideological squabbles, or perhaps one group had run into a government patrol, or else the soldiers were exorcising their fears by shooting at stray dogs, bats, and dead-drunk Cocambos.

The Chikraya was now perfectly still, straining to hear far-off sounds, perhaps, or already fast asleep. Not long before, she had surucated passionately in a way that was almost barbarous, brutal, practically suicidal, as if she'd wished to experience with Fabian, all at once, what she would normally have taken weeks or entire months to discover, or as if they'd been celebrating their reunion after endless separation, after years of blood and loneliness and a series of deaths. They hadn't said much; they hadn't felt the need of words to lose themselves in each other. At the moment when they'd exchanged smiles in the dim hotel lobby (in the entrance hall to that dubious place that had some connection with a hotel), at the moment when the lights had failed, they'd sealed a pact without need of language, and then that silent harmony had grown richer at each stage of their embrace: as she undressed, drawing him toward her, toward the bed completely veiled in shadows in the windowless room, and then as they lay interlaced, when she guided him inside her, opening to receive him, and then when they frolicked and sighed, taking their pleasure.

Fabian tried to shake off the hateful images of his nightmare, and his plaintive stillness must have betrayed some mute appeal, because the Chikraya whispered to him after a few minutes.

Tell me what you dreamed, my Jucapira.

He moved a bit closer to her, seeking the touch of her

breasts, her belly. He had no desire to summon up what hovered in the gloom around the edges of his memory.

He questioned her about the guerrillas and the sounds of battle.

Yes, she said. Probably one of the groups controlled by Pomponi.

Pomponi? he repeated.

I envy you—having no idea this person exists, sighed the Chikraya.

Spaced far apart, with long, inexplicable pauses, bursts of gunfire came and went in the night, over at the edge of town near the army post and the local dump. Since the electric generators had been sabotaged, the streets of Yaguatinga remained sunk in darkness beneath the opaque sky. A faint breeze drifted along the railroad tracks, scattering echoes of the fighting.

Tell me your dream, she said again.

Aside from two ventilation openings located up by the ceiling, there were no windows in the room.

The air was thick with dust.

Fabian changed position, clasping the Indian woman tightly. Her hair tumbled over him, pouring the scent of campfires across his face.

He kneaded her rounded shoulder, her dimpled arm; his hand wandered over her breasts and up to the yacaratia seeds of her ear ornament.

He was thinner than she was.

She wrapped her right leg around his legs.

They both had the vague impression that they had often, in the past, lain side by side like this and fallen asleep.

I dreamed that I was approaching the headwaters of the Abacau, and that I passed beyond them, he said. You won't find a single Indian there. Not even the Jabaanas flee that far. Not even the Cocambos. The pirogue was rocking. The water was strangely smooth and covered with floating weeds. I had reached a lake, a great lake. Dawn was about to break. I was trembling with fever. When I sifted through my thoughts to find out who I'd been, I came up with rubbish that had most likely belonged to other people. I was getting myself all filthy with these memories without understanding them. I knew that I'd been killed after a long interrogation, that they'd killed me on a river bank, that they'd killed me in the forest and then let me drift around in the marshes, that they'd killed me in the back of a courtyard and then thrown me into the water . . .

Don't get lost in details, said the Chikraya.

Her voice was hoarse, the way Indian women's voices often are after lovemaking.

Do you remember the legend of the Cobra Grande, of the Mother-of-all-waters, asked Fabian, the story of the snake that inhabits inexistence? I dreamed it was swimming toward me to put an end to my voyage at last. It was an immense anaconda. I was not afraid. Its head towered above the surface of the lake, and left no wake behind it in the weeds, the yellow algae.

I get the impression that you're making this up. That's not what you saw in your dream.

Yes, my little Chikraya, admitted Fabian. I'm making this up.

I know you by heart, said the Chikraya.

They stopped talking to make sure that the crackling noises and explosions were still coming from somewhere off near the army post, in other words, far from the hotel, streets and streets away.

Go on, tell me your dream, she urged him.

No, I'd rather make one up. Something terrible was happening to you in my nightmare and I couldn't do anything to prevent it. I was losing you.

She laughed, nibbling on the edge of his ear, the back of his neck.

I don't want to lose you anymore, even in a dream.

You're sweet, my Jucapira, said the Chikraya. I adore you.

11

WHILE THE pirogue in his dream rocked gently, he watched the pale cast of dawn spread across the sky, and at the same time, I saw the line of trees along the water's edge grow visible, and a flight of herons skimmed over the inert surface of things, followed by flamingos of a pink still untouched by the delicate tints of day.

All was calm, but one thing soothed me more than anything else: the certainty that I had already lived and dreamed this—the regular rocking of the canoe, the waiting, the lake beyond the headwaters of the river, at the source of the primeval ooze.

He listened to water without the tiniest ripple lapping against the side of the canoe. He opened his eyes. The humid air seemed to bring the nascent world more clearly into focus.

The colors growing lighter, brighter.

The vivid green of tender young branches already discernible here and there on the horizon.

Flamingos alighting on the gray tongue of a sand bar.

The immaculate sky. The last star barely visible.
I knew what would come next. Just beneath the surface, at
the bottom of the world, the Cobra Grande that is the
Mother-of-all-waters had emerged from its muddy bed and
was undulating slowly upward, guided by the reflections
of the morning above, spiraling toward the pirogue. The
serpent would claim me and return me to the primeval ooze
I'd had the unforgivable cheek to abandon on the day of
my birth.

Stop it, Golpiez! croaked Gonçalves in a rage. That's
enough! All this whining and self-pity!

He was gripping the dental chair, shaking it, choking with
effort.

My eyes were open! Wide open! continued Fabian, staring at the slide with the mystic gaze of a visionary.

The blue-gray dawn on the horizon was turning rosy, not
only to the east, as would have been logical, but everywhere,
all around me, as if the sun would soon appear simultane-
ously at all four points of the compass. In contrast, the trees
suddenly shrank into a sooty mass topped by the giant
crowns of imbaubas and assacus, which weren't so impressive, however, when viewed from offshore. The lake was car-
peted with water lilies and floating weeds. For one moment
I felt as though I were in the center of a vast clearing; then,
about forty yards away, something rose up that no storyteller
could ever describe, an anaconda of such size . . .

Shut up! barked Gonçalves.

The psychiatrist's intonation: like that used by someone
commanding dogs to be quiet.

The patient and the shaman darted glances at one
another. They sat scowling in silence; sweat began to bead
on their eyebrows, zigzagging steadily down their cheeks,
dampening their ocherous skin. Each felt like slapping the
other, and perhaps grabbing his hair and wrenching his

head back while looking around for a knife. Then the feeling melted away into the muggy atmosphere of the doctor's office without leaving behind even a trace of hostility or humiliation.

We'd known since the beginning that such moments of fleeting hatred would flare up between us, intense outbursts, inherent in the cure and thus destined to oblivion, purely therapeutic.

Gonçalves shrugged, rebuttoned his smock, and wiped his mouth. Spittle at the corners of his lips had thickened into a gray foam.

Do you think I'm some kind of idiot? he bellowed.

He flew into another fit. Perhaps it was only pretense; perhaps not.

These standard hallucinations! Vibrating canoes, anacondas! Old hat! Rivers fermenting beneath their cargo of leaves . . . The haunts of the Cobra Grande . . . What twaddle! Always the same junk! Sexual symbolism for half-wits!

There was a slight pause.

You thought you could fool me with trinkets, Golpiez! You were tossing me a dream to chew on!

Fabian listened silently to the other man's reproaches.

The session is over. Go on, cough up your last sentence without thinking it over, and then get out. You're beginning to annoy me.

I've known love only once in my life, said Fabian.

12

THEN SHE stretched out and wrapped herself more tightly, more snugly around him, as though she wanted to keep him from ever breaking free of her.

Then their faces drew close as their lips parted, searching...

Their mouths traveled together through the darkness. They swam from tongue to tongue, moist with saliva, oblivious to everything. They had never been separated since birth and so had always floated unctuously together.

He told her his name: Fabian, Fabian Golpiez. She caressed him, touching his cheek with great tenderness. He had as little beard as the other forest Indians she'd known, the Sobiberots, Curuçatins, Tangaras, Auguanis, Bacuras. Her fingers traced the angles of his jaw, slipped down his neck, and when they reached his clavicle, danced lightly along the curving bones. Then she whispered a name, her name: Leonor Nieves.

My little Chikraya, he said.

He had let the images of his nightmare fade away. In

his dream he'd seen the Chikraya murdered in the dark of night and carried off into the hills. They had interrogated her corpse for weeks, then sent it to the firing squad, again and again, finally heaving what was left of her into the water. They'd put her into the traditional pirogue with a small provision of rotten fruit. Fabian watched her being tortured but did not intervene; he couldn't bring himself to protest, or even to lie down in suffering and death beside the Chikraya. And then, later, when he'd finally decided to break free of the shame that paralyzed him and to endure the beatings and shootings, the Chikraya had vanished, or else she'd become monstrously disfigured and unrecognizable. Later—it was too late. So much for those images.

He shifted his elbow, drawing the smelly blanket around the two of them, and dreamily repeated: Leonor Nieves, Leonor Nieves.

There was nothing new in this name, which he had cherished from his first moment of life, of consciousness.

And even for much longer than that.

He had been that woman's lover since time began, since the world was born.

My little Chikraya, he said, come live with me. I've been posted to a civilian job in Mapiaupi. I'll be working in the hospital as a male nurse. We could live together, if you're free.

Leonor Nieves didn't reply. He heard and felt her breathing as she lay pressed against him. Closing his eyes, he inhaled her scent, the smell of leaves in the night air, and their common odors of sweat and dew and various amorous liquors.

Don't go to Mapiaupi by train, she whispered.

The road's been dynamited, he said. The bus can't get through anymore.

The train will be attacked between Yaguatinga and Mapiaupi, she explained in a deep, throaty voice, reluctantly, as if betraying a secret. I don't want you to be massacred, Fabianito.

At that instant, a powerful grenade exploded near the barracks, over where the government troops and the guerrillas were still fighting. The reverberations rolled through the streets between the clay-walled houses and along the railroad tracks. A pane of glass rattled on the front door.

Everything magical or poetic or exhilarating in the air they were breathing disappeared, as though swept away by that sound wave. Their nostrils were filled with the fustiness of a room that was never cleaned, a foul-smelling place where the tattered wretches of the civil war sought shelter, in a hotel with shabby beds and revolting blankets and kerosene lamps without any kerosene.

Did you hear that? murmured the Chikraya.

Her lips.

Her warm legs on mine.

The anxiety in her voice.

Yes, said Fabian. A grenade. One of the cottage industries of the revolution. Don't worry. They're far away.

Nights at the front had taught him that—how to read those blasts in the dark void, the messages of metal, the howling of murder.

But now they will come closer, said the Chikraya.

13

ANOTHER SESSION.

In October, perhaps. Let's say in October.

I sat in the dental chair in apathetic silence and watched Gonçalves fill out the medical history sheet I had to hand in every week to the health department, a document certifying that I had a very poor grasp of reality, a view of the world and the revolution barely distinguishable from that of a Cocambo, and a sense of self so muddled that it was still too soon to assign me a job or authorize the political security forces to summon me back to the Calle 19 de Febrero for further interrogation.

It's not getting any better, observed Gonçalves.

I didn't know whether he was referring to my illness or to the sultry weather. He seemed less crabby than usual that day. I could vaguely make him out behind the flower pots on his desk, sitting amid the vines that had woven rope bridges all around the room, from the furniture to the shelves to the window blinds.

He looked up at me with the eyes of a myopic raptor; the

irises had nice gold flecks in them, but they'd been tarnished by age. Everything else about his face was hideous. The masklike features of elderly Jucapiras, as I said before, tend to be spectacularly ugly. I'm preparing myself psychologically to resemble him. We are both pure Jucapiras, and none of our tribe escapes this fate.

You don't eat enough fruit, he remarked in a pleasant and quite unfamiliar tone. Your color's bad, Golpiez. The pigment in your skin seems to have begun leaching away from the inside. You're turning yellow. And do you know why? Because you're stuffing yourself with toads and reptiles in the company of your friend Gutiérrez. You want to make him believe you have an Indian appetite and a digestive system that's one hundred percent Indian. A typically Jucapira inferiority complex. Result: your stomach's eating itself up with gangrene. Am I right?

I gestured evasively.

Eat more fruit, insisted Gonçalves. Stay away from tortoise, iguana, snake, frog, lizard.

And avoid roast monitor, he added.

Those words, I said. Those imperialist names. When you have the dentist's glossary at your fingertips!

Gonçalves ignored my reproach. He initialed my certificate of schizophrenia, handed it to me, and began choosing the slides intended to prod my memory.

I went to pull the raffia mats over the windows. Outside, the fog hadn't lifted. Unwholesome mists drifted among the tree trunks. Not a single creature could be seen. Moisture dripped silently from the vegetation.

When I returned to my seat, the magic lantern was already lit. The psychiatrist continued to select slides and stack them up in front of him.

Hmm, he exclaimed softly to himself.

What is it? I asked.

A photo of the dentist.

Your predecessor?

Yes. That legendary man, the one who collected the names of monkeys and ants in the common tongue. By the way, he was probably no more a dentist than you and I are.

What do you know about him?

Not much. The local authorities requisitioned his office, which I inherited. They must have told me his story, but I've forgotten it.

I raised my voice; switching roles seemed a simple matter, and I got carried away.

Why don't we take a look at his picture? I cried. Why don't you show us something instead of inflicting your amnesia on us?

Gonçalves inserted the slide into the viewer, which clattered and threw upon the wall the image of a man in shorts and a white sports shirt, wearing a bush hat and lovingly clutching a revolutionary's machine gun. His tawny Jucapira eyes possessed a certain charm. He was not smiling for the camera.

I'm listening, I said.

I can't remember anymore, groaned Gonçalves.

You don't have to speak in the first person, I said.

Thank goodness for that.

Get on with it! I bawled.

One fine day, began Gonçalves, this fellow slipped the key under the door and vanished into the forest. Without a word of warning. Unremitting nostalgia for the revolution, as well as weariness at having to spend entire afternoons sniffing the pestilential stink of his patients' rotting mouths. Dentistry was not his original specialty, of course. The local council must have assigned him here to test him, or because the post was available, but whatever the case, he was never fascinated by impacted molars, or crooked canines, or abscessed roots, or gums like mushroom beds. None of that gave him any pleasure. For a while he'd tried to amuse himself by collecting objects of the forest culture, native weapons, and then he'd collected words, jotting down the rudiments of a dictionary of the vernacular, lists he learned by heart and recited over at the Calle 19 de Febrero when the Auguanis voiced doubts about the Indian nature of his identity. Like all Jucapiras, in fact, he was constantly challenged by the Indians to prove that he belonged to their community, while the revolutionaries challenged him as well to prove that he belonged to theirs.

We know, we know, I said.

But boredom got the best of him in the end. He jumped into a pirogue and paddled upriver. The house stayed empty for a long time. Plants crept in through the windows to blanket everything. Now it's a villa in ruins, home to the worst snakes in the region . . .

Which ones? I grunted. One might think you were incapable of giving them their Indian names.

Jararacas. Jibóias, ibiraquas, urutus. And boiuçus. Japaranas as well. And I'm leaving some out. And, luckily, muçuranas, which like to eat the others.

You're getting things mixed up with your dreams! I protested. This place isn't as infested as all that.

Oh yes it is! shouted the psychiatrist, waving his arms. It's easy to see you don't live here! Day and night, coiling and uncoiling everywhere! Hissing at my ankles when I stumble! Casting their skins all over the place! I live in a scaly madhouse! Clearly you . . .

All right, if you say so, I agreed.

Up on the wall, the tooth puller kept a tight grip on his machine gun, clasping it affectionately to his belly.

Where were we, Gonçalves—ah yes, the dentist. The itinerary of his flight.

The forest covers all tracks, said Gonçalves.

Improvise, I suggested. Pretend you are speaking of yourself.

He goes to join the guerrillas who roamed the upper reaches of the Abacau and the Retiete, said Gonçalves. For ten or fifteen years he accompanies one band or another, without ever decisively joining one particular faction, which might suggest that he is affiliated with some secret organization, with the Bandera or its police, but in fact he is simply prone to insubordination. In the end, he is executed by a firing squad. They put his bullet-riddled corpse into a canoe. He travels through the flooded rain forest, through noxious marshes, through the realms of spiders. Then he lives in abandoned Cocambo villages, opening a clinic for Cocambos and Jabaanas, making himself useful. Later he turns up at the head of a column of antigovernment troops on the Yaguari, and he leads several internationalist campaigns. Arrested again, he disappears again, and this time for years. Then he returns to Puesto Libertad. They do not allow him time enough to add even a few pages to his dictionary. He goes directly from the wharf to the Calle 19 de Febrero, where he is eliminated once and for all. He is interrogated through and through, and eliminated for good.

The shaman-doctor swallowed hard.

That fate awaits us all, Golpiez, he said.

Then it was my turn to swallow hard.

Your fears are absurd and counterrevolutionary, I said. Neurotic phobias! But it doesn't matter. Let's continue.

Very well, let's continue! he said, with a sudden note of menace in his voice.

He had just shifted the track of the slide viewer.

Like a soldier roughly ejecting an empty cartridge casing from the magazine of his rifle.

That sharp sound.

The dentist and his nonsmile were gone.

Close parenthesis, Golpiez, announced the psychiatrist. We're switching roles again. Got that?

Yes, I sighed.

The next slide showed a rectangular, one-story building with a broken ticket window and a facade completely pockmarked by bullet holes. I recognized the place; my fingers tightened convulsively on the armrests of the dental chair.

Yaguatinga, I stammered. The train station.

You remember?

Yes, but show the hotel. Show the hotel instead.

Gonçalves projected the next slide: an unfinished, windowless building, its walls surmounted by what were intended to have become terraces.

The hotel at night, I murmured. The picture should be much darker. You shouldn't be able to see a thing. There was no light at all in the room. Show the room. Show the night.

Then I was silent. Searching for words.

None came.

Improvise, said Gonçalves.

14

SO, YAGUATINGA.

Its wretched little houses huddled along the unlit streets.
The railroad tracks slicing ominously through the town.
Those dull, lusterless rails: that promise of a dark voyage.
The bursts of automatic-weapons fire, and every so often,
a grenade.

From a military point of view, the situation had changed.
A commando unit was now advancing determinedly from
intersection to intersection, forcing the government troops
to retreat.

The army patrol had at first set up a barrier on the outskirts of town, but the guerrillas had dislodged the soldiers,
who now found themselves too far from the army post to
expect any tactical support from that quarter and so were
ceding ground, fighting more and more poorly as they
went. Their resistance was sporadic, half-hearted.

The guerrillas were gradually advancing toward the station.

There are five or six of them, and they're coming closer,
whispered the Chikraya.

She shifted her position on the mattress. Her anxiety was almost palpable.

Small arms, said Fabian. What are you afraid of, my little Chikraya? We're safe from the bullets.

I'm the one they're after, said Leonor Nieves.

You?

He tried to touch her, to take her hand, but she eluded his grasp.

Pomponi must have agreed to have me liquidated, she said.

She slipped barefoot across the cement floor.

That's just his style, she continued. Suggesting a place where I could hole up beyond their reach, organizing my journey, and at the same time supporting a night attack to capture or simply murder me.

She'd begun searching under the bed, in the blanket lying on the floor, pushing aside her bag and Fabian's pack. She gathered her clothes. The kerosene lamp rolled farther away. The empty copper fuel reservoir scraped across bits of stone debris.

Listen, Fabianito, I'm not crazy, said the Chikraya. I haven't time to explain, and anyway you're like all the Jucapiras—you don't understand a thing about the revolution. They want to liquidate me because they imagine that I'm collaborating secretly with the Bandera.

Scenes of violence and pursuit resurfaced in Fabian's memory. He had already dreamed this, or something like it. The crackle of machine guns fell silent, then began again; the sound was growing clearer all the time.

You're a member of the Bandera? he asked.

The Chikraya was dressing quickly in the dark. Before she put them on, she shook out her blouse, her skirt, as though she were thinking, despite her haste, about what might now be clinging to the material after its stay under the bed: dust, wood lice, little yellow scorpions.

You know, she replied evasively, the Bandera manipulates everything that moves, in the government troops as well as in the guerrilla forces.

She had finished dressing. She listened intently.

They're not far away anymore, she murmured.

She felt her way around the bed and to Fabian's nude body, to his face, the face of a Jucapira who had such trouble understanding things. She leaned over and kissed him. In her hand was a good-sized gun, and without his clothes, Fabian seemed like a child whom a grown woman was cajoling affectionately for a few moments before going off to work or prison or war.

Wait for me, he said. I'm coming with you.

He groped around in the tangled blankets and the absolute darkness for his trousers, underpants, shirt. He couldn't find a thing.

It's you who are going to wait for me, Fabianito, said the Chikraya. You don't know anything about this business, so don't get mixed up in it. I'm going to disappear. Tomorrow, go to Mapiaupi via the river. At the hospital, you'll find someone sympathetic to our cause. Manda. A nurse in the psychiatric department. As soon as I can, I'll send you a message through her.

All physical contact between them was already gone. She crossed the room. She reached the door. She opened it without a sound.

She crouched down, speculating about the gunfire crackling out in the streets. She must have held her pistol at the ready. She must have been thinking that it would be difficult to leave through the front door, because men were already running in front of the train station opposite the hotel.

The government troops were fleeing, firing the occasional round at their pursuers. One of the soldiers could be heard galloping heavily. Others were zigzagging along the railroad tracks.

That labored breathing.

That headlong dash, hugging the line of colorless houses.

The Chikraya had left the room. Fabian heard the faint creaking of a door, perhaps the one to the courtyard.

On the little square in front of the station, different footsteps could be heard. The commandos had reached their objective and were deploying around the hotel.

The machine-gun fire had ceased.

Fabian stood up and wandered about the room, blindly, uselessly, with his arms stretched out in front of him. His bare feet trod on gravel, cruddy wads of hair, stalks of dry grass, scattered scraps of rancid food.

He returned to the bed and sat down again.

There were new developments outside. Whisperings, comings and goings. A brief command. Then men entered the building, stopping warily at the beginning of the corridor. Fabian could imagine them on the other side of the wall. They were suspicious, focused on the possible presence of the enemy, attentive to anything unnatural in the silence.

Fabian kept still now, sitting passively on a corner of the mattress, listening.

He tried to breathe calmly.

Then, as in his dream, someone kicked in the door. It slammed into the wall and swung closed again, screeching on its hinges; then, propelled by a fresh but slightly less savage kick, it banged into the cinder blocks once more.

The door was wide open, yet not even the faintest tinge of gray had appeared in the cavernous night.

Leonor Nieves! called a gruff voice.

Fabian did nothing. It was doubtless best to let the man waste time on the wrong track. After a moment, the man spoke again.

Leonor Nieves?

Then a flashlight beam pierced the darkness, disclosing Fabian stark naked in the center of the desolate room.

Rough cement walls, their uneven surface clotted with ugly shadows; blankets all in a heap; clothing lying across two canvas packs or crumpled on the floor—that's what the light suddenly revealed.

And that astonished Jucapira, just sitting there blinking.

His penis: mauve, yellow.

The Indian switched off the flashlight; the last thing in its beam had been a cockroach, also yellow. The inspection hadn't lasted very long or occasioned any commentary, either from the man with the flashlight or the two Coariguaçus accompanying him. The three men piled into the room, thinking to shield themselves from the bullets of anyone lying in ambush up ahead. They hunched down at the doorway, motionless, invisible again, turning their backs on that shameless Jucapira who could do them no harm. They considered carefully every little message floating by: the pungency of chicken droppings, infinitesimal variations of temperature, the soft whistle of the draft. Then they went back out into the corridor.

The Indian with the flashlight was in charge.

Here, he murmured. To the right. I'll go. Now, the one across from us. On the left.

One after the other, the doors to the shabby rooms flew open, crashed into the wall, and swung back, moaning and grating. The flashlight would gleam for a moment; the men would point their guns at whatever they saw in that fraction of a second. Then utter darkness would return. The hotel was empty. No one was lurking among the cockroaches, amid the construction rubbish, hiding on or under the beds with their disgusting straw mattresses.

The three men put their heads together. They did not

seem unduly discouraged by their initial lack of success. They could be heard whispering.

There's a courtyard, and more rooms.

She's out there.

She's definitely out there, in the courtyard.

The group had crept down to the end of the hall. The door to the patio was next; it was heavier, not as easy to force suddenly because it opened toward the inside. This door banged, creaked, and then, as in a fit of delirium when hallucinations repeat themselves endlessly and without mercy, the Indian in command stuck his head into the courtyard and yelled . . .

Leonor Nieves?

But this time, he got his answer: a bullet just over his nose, right between the eyes.

15

I STOPPED. I couldn't go on.

I didn't want to look at those slides anymore. Gonçalves had been projecting me in those slides for hours. I was blinded by sweat. I closed my eyes. Tearing myself away from Yaguatinga, from that night.

Don't stop, said Gonçalves. What do you see now? What's going on inside you? Leonor Nieves—what's happening to her inside you?

I just sat there.

Talk, Golpiez!

Whistling and shrieking over Puesto Libertad swoop the guandiras, giant bats with a wingspan of up to two yards. They wait until dusk to appear; then they follow the Avenida Bandera downtown to the Bulevar Insurrección del 28 de Enero, where they swing round, their monstrous wings brushing against the trees of the park in front of a block of office buildings. Flapping onward, they drift off to the Plaza Mártires del 12 de Abril, and picking up speed above the Calle 19 de Febrero, they return to the Avenida Bandera, which they descend at one go, although they sometimes make a detour to fly over the Calle 30 de Abril, and the huts of the Cocambos, and the hut where I live. When they're dead center over the wharf, they slap the humid air with a vast membranous smack and speed along the Embarcadero Fusilados del 31 de Agosto toward the slum called Manuela Aratuípe. They soar back and forth over us like that, hunting in some way difficult to understand: whistling, wheeling between two breezes, screaking those shrill sounds that penetrate the eardrums to attack our most deeply buried memories.

You hear these disquieting cries, and the leathery thwack of their abrupt turns.

And then? asked Gonçalves.

And then, nothing, I replied.

I opened my eyes. The office was filled with the greenish mist of a waning afternoon. Behind the plants, Gonçalves was glumly gathering together his shaman's paraphernalia. The session hadn't shed much light on anything, and it was already time for me to come up with my final sentence.

When you hear those cries, that flapping, I stammered, you know that twilight has arrived.

16

LATER.

The end of October, or perhaps it was already November. It was late, I'm certain of that.

My position: stretched out next to Manda.

The shadows off in the corners of the dilapidated shack were blooming like flowers. Manda was stroking my back, my lower back. Slowly. Her hand explored between my legs: the hairs, the elastic masses, flaccid or semifirm.

Had you surucated? asked a voice.

I'd come to see Manda, the way I always do on Saturdays. We'd taken our pleasure, such as it was—an Indian man and woman already slowed down by age and physical lassitude, and long past taking an interest in living or even in pretending to engage in any organic activity whatsoever.

Skip the fancy stuff, ordered the voice.

Suddenly, however, I wanted to surucate one more time, to hold Manda in my arms so that I could forget everything else, to be as one with her, inside her.

You're still the same, I told her. You haven't picked up a

single wrinkle, not one, in all those years since we lived together in Mapiaupi. You haven't changed, my little Chikraya.

Stop your silliness, Fabianito, my little madman, said Manda, pushing me away. And let me remind you that I'm a Cayacoe, not a Chikraya.

She was laughing.

For a few minutes, we reminisced about the years in Mapiaupi, the revolution in Mapiaupi, our apartment, situated so unhealthily close to the river, near the Cocambo neighborhood, and then we started talking about the intrigues and love affairs that had occasionally stirred up trouble between us.

That last year, said Manda, you hardly had any opportunity to notice whether or not I had any wrinkles. You were running after María Gabriela.

She shook her head, smiling.

That lasted such a short time, I said.

You were chasing after her like an idiotic dog, tongue hanging out, nose twitching, and that's not the half of it. It took months for you to figure out the kind of bitch she could be.

Keep your voice down, I warned her. You never know.

Since it was growing dark out, toads had begun croaking heartily all around the hut, without managing, however, to drown out other noises in the garden: the rustle of damp grass, and cautious breathing, quite close. Someone was crouched in the bushes, his ear pressed to the other side of the planks, a few inches from where we were chatting.

I've always hated that slut, continued Manda. I don't see why I shouldn't say it as loud as I please. She had enough people shot in Mapiaupi to prove what she's really like. I'm not going to keep quiet just because she's in charge of Puesto Libertad now.

I pointed to the wall on which our heads were leaning. The toads were belching rhythmically. A man had stepped a few yards away to cough. You could already hear him returning.

Don't worry, Fabianito, whispered Manda. It's Gutiérrez out hunting monitors or iguanas. I recognize his way of sniffing.

I kissed Manda. For thirty seconds we pretended to press on, lips to lips and legs entwined. Then Manda got winded. She has circulation problems. I'm not as robust as I used to be, either. My heart was beating unevenly, and I felt a sort of numbness in my limbs, the kind that . . .

Spare me your health bulletin until I ask you for it, said the voice impatiently.

I recognized Gonçalves and fell silent. I don't know why, but he doesn't like hearing me speak tenderly of Manda— he hates the scenes where I share her bed. He seeks the slightest pretext to interrupt me and tries to get me talking about things in the background instead.

Night was falling, prompted the voice.

I didn't say another word.

Finish the sequence, commanded the voice. We have the sound effects, the giant guandiras squeaking over Puesto Libertad, the batrachians burping crepuscularly among the nettles, the informer clearing his throat. Now add some more picturesque details and let's get on with it.

I was thinking of Manda. I would have liked to bring her back onstage.

I remained silent for half a minute. The light was failing.

For example, the evening spider, prodded the voice. The evening insects.

In an attempt to drive off Gutiérrez, I banged my fist against the boards right where his ear was glued. A tarantula disturbed by my blows lost its balance and rolled down between Manda and me. We could make out its handful of nervous legs on the mattress, the uneasy velvet of its body. I immediately folded a strip of raffia matting over it and pressed down grimly, but without encountering the usual crunching resistance.

You missed it, said Manda. Go light the lamp, Fabianito. I want to find out where it's hiding.

I rushed for the lamp. Smoke from the coconut oil rose to perfume the air. Holding the lantern out in front of me, I moved the bed, the pillows of dried grasses, the blanket. Manda went back and forth in the hut.

An unorganized and unsuccessful hunt.

Afterward we calmed down.

Too bad, said Manda. We can live with it.

She straightened up the table where we'd eaten early in the afternoon. Some lukewarmish water gurgled in the bottom of a pitcher. She drank half of it and handed the rest to me. We were both naked and streaming with sweat, two savages illuminated by the dim light from that wretched coconut oil.

All right, all right, said the voice. One last detail and that's it.

There were many insects that night. The air was fraying into scraps of mist laden with moths and mosquitoes. The bold ones would buzz around the lamp wick, sizzle, and then continue—despite their singeing—to loop ever more acrobatic loops, incapable of realizing that they'd already been mortally wounded by the flame.

Fine, that's it, said the voice.

17

ANOTHER TIME. Another session in November. Everything had already been recited in fantastic detail and gone
into thoroughly from all angles and scrutinized and peered
at in black and white and held up to the light and drama-
tized and exorcised with great recourse to slides or ritual
forest artifacts or stomatological implements. Outside
the office windows, crickets and beetles and dwarfish
monkeys and parrots were saluting the end of a month
of rain by shrieking louder and louder. Gonçalves was turning up the volume as well. Every so often, on the other
hand, disheartened by the conditions of this uncertain
contest, we'd stop shouting, content to murmur amid the
triumphant and omnipresent greenery, off in our respec-
tive corners, each of us going through the motions of a session without taking the other one into account, chattering
away in a seagreen fog.

Actually, numerous topics hadn't been touched on or
broached or even hinted at, and through inertia we would
return, day after day, to subjects that no longer concealed

any pitfalls and awakened only pain that was familiar, accepted, without surprises. Well, almost without surprises.

Gonçalves was lounging behind the clusters of white orchids that had flowered on his desk. I could barely see him.

So, this Chikraya, this Leonor Nieves, he said.

Yes, I replied.

It all happened in absolute darkness.

The man formerly in charge of the operation—the man who had trained his flashlight on hordes of motionless cockroaches and called in vain the name of Leonor Nieves— had been annihilated with a single bullet.

At the moment of his instantaneous dismissal, he had fallen against the door, and his combat jacket had caught on a bolt, on some nails, keeping his body from complete collapse and even retaining a kind of dignity in his posture. Although he had dropped the flashlight and his weapon, he still seemed to be holding on, standing firm. The hinges creaked. He clung to the door with the stubbornness that only a corpse can show.

This leader with his brains blown out was something of a hindrance to the other two commandos. Each in turn bumped into the plank sticking up across the threshold and blindly sent a burst of gunfire roaring into the courtyard, demolishing the slats of the rabbits' and guinea pigs' cages and sowing panic among the poultry.

The thunderous echoes died away.

The sky was a black cut-out atop the black walls of the patio.

The guinea pigs yapped in endless, hopeless terror. Chickens and guinea fowl cackled frantically. It seemed highly likely that some of this diminutive livestock had been perforated by the odd bullet, for little creatures could be heard sobbing. There was no longer a single sound of human origin in this part of the hotel.

Fabian collected his scattered clothing, piece by piece. Out in the corridor, the two survivors panted with fear. Without a weapon, it was pointless to try attacking them from behind. Fabian dressed slowly, concentrating his thoughts on Leonor Nieves, on his memory of her. Perhaps she had escaped via a terrace, under the cover of that terrific din. Perhaps she was already far away, dashing from one pool of shadows to another, slipping down alleyways leading her closer and closer to safety.

In reality, there had not been enough time for Leonor Nieves to find a way out of the courtyard. She was hiding behind a pile of bricks, near the sink, between the latrines and the rabbit hutch. She was watching the doorway to the corridor, a dark slot stuffed with a hulking body.

Aside from this passageway with its corpse and armed Coariguaçus, there was no way to reach the outside without performing feats of acrobatics. The rooms giving onto the patio had openings that were supposed to become doors and windows some day, but they were all on the interior side, as though intended to create guest accommodations that resembled solitary confinement, without any communication with the street. The rare skylights were equipped with iron bars.

The Indian woman considered the stacks of cages. She could clamber up on them, hold onto a concrete pillar, and leap to a terrace, or the roof. There she'd have more freedom of movement. She would crawl out of sight and, with any luck, sneak clean away.

In any case, such a climb would be noisy and would take a few moments. The guerrillas waiting in ambush behind their dead leader would hurry out and have ample time to direct a hail of bullets at her, shredding her body, her mind, her memories of love and revolution.

She reached out and shook the guinea pigs' cage, as

though she had hurled herself into the dangerous ascent. Just as she had foreseen, someone pushed aside the bothersome corpse and showed his face in the doorway. She recognized him, remembered his first name, Pedro, and his age, twenty-three, and she sent him a sharp, slashing message just under his chin, something to do with a voyage, with the beginning or the end of a voyage. Leonor Nieves was a good shot. Pedro knelt, then tipped over. In his fall he tore his dead companion loose from the bolt and the nails supporting him. Then Pedro began to gasp and agonize in a voice like the gurgling of a baby.

His moans were easily lost in the horrified uproar of the chickens, but if you listened carefully, you could just make them out.

Leonor Nieves listened to the life spurting out of Pedro, and the rabbits, and the guinea pigs, more and more quietly. She rattled the cage again. Before going up on the roof, she had to get rid of the third guerrilla, lurking in the hallway. She had to lure him out of hiding and kill him.

For some unknown reason, the sky of the Guaraiti, which in that season is usually a river of diamonds, had refused for hours now to shed light on the world below.

The Chikraya peered into the gloom, riveting her gaze on the dead angle behind which the last Coariguaçu had to be hiding. She did not raise her eyes often enough to the night sky. And suddenly she realized that in that absence of stars, something had moved, shifted a yard or so, flattening out. Up on a terrace. Out of sight and out of range. The constant cackling kept her from determining the precise spot where this additional opponent was stretched out, breathing.

She began to slip silently along the rabbit hutch, looking for a place where she would be less vulnerable, but saw none. She retreated toward the sink, the latrines. With the barrel of her pistol she traced the indistinct shapes looming over the courtyard: heaps of broken tiles, the beginnings of a low wall, rubble and ruins without any coherence. She saw no one.

Calm returned gradually to the patio. Exhausted, the animals were quiet. On the threshold of the door to the hallway, Pedro had breathed his last.

Next to Leonor Nieves, a faucet dripped into an iron box. The smell from the chicken coop grew even sharper. It was hard to decide which was worse, the stink of poultry splattered with blood and dung, or the reek of the latrines.

Nothing was happening.

No one started anything; it was better not to betray one's position by risking a shot.

Fabian held his breath. He remained motionless in the room, as though he, too, were taking part in the fight.

Then, as in his dream, things happened quickly, and it was all over.

Without warning, a powerful fusillade broke out. The man in the corridor unleashed long salvos that once more pounded the fragile rampart protecting Leonor Nieves and once more pierced wings, combs, muzzles, silken bellies. Two machine guns spat fire from the terraces, seeking to annihilate anything resembling an armed shadow at the back of the courtyard.

An iron box rolled along the cement slab near the latrines.

The Indian woman was aiming at the sky.

When the salvos ended, she got off one more shot, one wild, pathetic shot.

There was a silence, followed by exclamations in the vernacular, in Coariguaçu and Auguani, and then footsteps over Fabian's room. A man was running from terrace to terrace, cracking pieces of tile beneath his boots.

Now that man stood boldly at the edge of the roof, examining what lay sprawled backward across a wheelbarrow full of bricks amid the wreckage of the cages. Without taking any special precautions, he studied what little could be seen. Then he let off one last burst of fire.

18

SOMETHING DIFFERENT, said the psychiatrist.
A different ending to the session. Then I'll let you go.

Gonçalves had taken down from the wall a glittering crown fashioned from the plumage of forest birds, one of the loveliest pieces in the dentist's collection. Carrying out his duties as a shaman, he now began to shake this crown of feathers all around me.

What birds? he asked. What are they called? It's hard to tell what forest you mean or what language you're jabbering in.

There were tail feathers from a toucan, said Fabian. From a toucan, yes, and feathers from a sanhaçu...from an ara-bira, a bright-eyed sassy . . . a guiratirica . . .

The commotion in the office was reaching a climax. Gonçalves brandished the rainbow-colored headpiece on high, and then, performing a Cocambo dance step, he brought it abruptly down between his face and that of Fabian, where he made it tremble and then jerk convulsively, as if he wanted to claw the humid air and punctuate the exchange of bellowed questions and answers with the musty smell of poultry.

Fabian stiffened in the dental chair. The mechanical arm-piece kept bumping into his right shoulder. The brilliant red feathers of the ornament were shedding equatorial grubs, gelatinous cocoons, semihatched eggs that were already aggressive.

Give us something more substantial! trumpeted Gonçalves. You're just spinning out your old traumas! There's no plot, no structure to your stories!

Fabian coughed. He was suffocating amid the stinking wisps of down. He sized up his tormentor with a vindictive eye. The crown of mostly red and yellow feathers was still scattering segmented gray parasites and tiny barbed cater-pillars in all directions.

This stuff you're giving me is all trash! exclaimed Gonçalves indignantly. You were saying, one evening in Yaguatinga . . . Returning from the front . . . You'd started to tell a story . . . Yaguatinga, the station, the hotel! You were telling me that an Indian woman, a Chikraya . . .

A pathetic affair! cried Fabian, brushing off the mess that had rained down on him. A pretty lousy excuse for an adventure, Doctor! A furtive encounter at the hotel! I never even saw that woman! It all happened in the dark! She never told me her name! We didn't talk in bed, we just slept together, without a word, and I fell asleep right after-ward . . . At dawn she'd already disappeared!

He was gasping.

Speak up! brayed Gonçalves. Speak clearly!

Nothing more! screamed Fabian. Nothing important! A one-night stand at a station hotel . . . A quiet night!

And then, brought dramatically back to life by Gonçalves, a fabulous bird fluttered up into the air, a magical tou-can that plunged and twirled before Fabian's teary eyes.

Feigning a desire to land on his face or chest, it sprinkled tiny plumules on those lips smudged with the dust of words or lies; then it went suddenly into a nose dive, as if attacking the psychiatrist's knees just above the hem of his white smock or even lower, where his bare legs exposed to the dim light the wounds and ulcers of incurable Indian diseases. The toucan would beat its wings frantically, shoot aloft, and let out a cry very like a mocking sob before swooping downward once again.

II

MUD

19

IN DECEMBER, my comfy daily routine of nonexistence began to go off track.

First of all, the Auguanis at the Calle 19 de Febrero started summoning Gonçalves to their premises again. When I arrived for my appointments at the usual times, I would often find the office closed. Although I knew no one would answer the door, I'd swat stubbornly at the jingling bell hanging beneath the doctor's nameplate. I needed to talk about my memories, needed desperately to lie to an Indian who would help bolster my protestations of unflinching loyalty to the revolutionary cause or my claims of belonging to the Indian community. I wanted another look at the slides illustrating what had haunted me before my death. My vocabulary was suffering, too, and I was anxious to get my hands on the lists of words compiled by the dentist.

I walked around the house that had once been the home of the legendary tooth puller, an internationalist, a Jucapira internationalist, like Gonçalves and myself. I couldn't get close to the windows because of the dense vegetation; snakes hissed at me as I passed. I came full circle, reached for the little bell, made myself dizzy with its jangling, distressed that the ringing within would awaken only poisonous jararacas or boas.

I read Gonçalves's nameplate aloud, as though that summons would possess the shaman's power to whisk my psychiatrist away from the clutches of the political security forces.

FABIAN GONÇALVES
FORMER CHIEF PSYCHIATRIST, VETERANS' HOSPITAL OF JUAUPES
PSYCHOLOGIST, SOCIAL SERVICES DEPARTMENT OF
PUESTO LIBERTAD

The hospital in Juaupes! sputtered Rui Gutiérrez, official veteran. Baloney! A complete fraud! You won't find Juaupes on a single map!

It's beyond the source of the Abacau, I said, shocked by his tone, by his constant need to disparage Gonçalves.

There aren't any maps of the headwaters of the Retiete and the Abacau, insisted Gutiérrez. That region is unexplored. May I remind you that we will be the first to go there, Golpiez. Remember that.

I know. I haven't forgotten. The psychiatric clinic for Cocambos and Jabaanas. The foundation of a utopian community. I haven't forgotten.

He lurched, his breath horribly warmed by fermented blood and juices, and began a new diatribe against Gonçalves. He had pulled some lizards and catfish from his knapsack. I scaled and cut them up in silence. I was sulking.

I was brooding over what had recently gone wrong with my routine, my life in Puesto Libertad.

So: early in December they'd started interrogating

Gonçalves down on the Calle 19 de Febrero. Due to his repeated absences, the number of sessions I was able to complete dropped significantly. The health authorities therefore concluded that I was refusing my prescribed treatment, and they cut off my benefits without any warning. I learned in mid-month that I had been dropped from the list of disabled veterans. I learned this from the judge's assessor himself, in his second-floor office at the Calle 19 de Febrero. He had my dossier spread out all over the table. With great pleasure, the assessor read me the latest slips added to my file. I had lost the immunity I'd enjoyed as a psychotic with severe and intractable disabilities. The Auguani made a point of deciphering before me two notes handwritten by Gonçalves, one dating from September or October and containing a diagnosis of my disorder for the local authorities, while the other—much more recent, doubtless obtained during an interrogation down in the kitchen courtyard—stated that although I possessed an innate tendency toward schizophrenic ravings, I displayed, on the whole, the mentality and attitudes of a malingerer.

And that, remarked the assessor, made my situation in Puesto Libertad even more precarious than it had been at the beginning of the summer—extremely delicate, in fact, and liable to collapse overnight.

My harassment by the authorities began again: long waits, squatting in the courtyard; demands for information followed by mock executions; pummelings against the palisade in back; confrontations with the victims, with what was about to be hacked up by Auguani machetes and tossed on the grill.

When I had a free afternoon, I went to see Gonçalves to continue my analysis. I was under no further official obligation to do so, but I went to sit in that dental chair because I could no longer do without the psychiatrist's shouting and dancing around. Probing my mutilations and wounds so deeply with Gonçalves, I could enjoy the illusion of having once lived elsewhere than in the present, in this unspeakable present. As for Gonçalves, he complained constantly. The maltreatment he was suffering at the hands of the Auguanis made him peevish. He no longer trotted out his therapeutic slides, and he questioned me more roughly now. He was drawing inspiration for this new style from the interrogations he himself was undergoing. His method had evolved: pleading increasing deafness as an excuse, he hollered in my ear and forced me to yell louder than anyone in that dental chair ever had before. We snarled at each other like an old couple going through menopause or divorce.

Yet fate had sent us sliding down similar slopes; more and more often, we staggered or wheezed in neighboring offices or courtyards at exactly the same time, which ought to have brought us closer together instead of driving us apart. For example, we might have discussed ways to withstand interrogation techniques featuring the slaughter of jacarés or the dismemberment of giant tortoises; we might at least have taken the occasional break from our therapeutic exertions to tell anecdotes about this or that Auguani inquisitor, thus creating a more relaxed atmosphere. But between us now reigned hostility and a distrust poisoned by what Rui Gutiérrez had forced me to see and hear, after having already made me crawl through the iguana-infested backyards of the Calle Escalante.

In December, Gutiérrez treated me to several demeaning revelations of this sort.

The first one enlightened me about Manda's private life and the company she kept.

The second one stunned me. It concerned Leonor Nieves.

The rest will be related in due course. It stunned me as well, but did not enlighten me. I found no light there at all; only obscurity and excrement.

20

THE IGUANA gardens of the Calle Escalante, around
Manda's hut. The plants favored by iguanas and monitors:
guaraquiás, tapirapecús, taramiaranas, and tajabembas,
among others. The plant names are not important. Grasses,
nettles. That's the decor through which we would soon be
creeping. But only when the twilight had faded.

For the moment, I'd just emerged from the headquarters
of the political security forces. My neck was bruised, my
head lolling, the way one's head is at sunset after an interrogation. I looked like a sleepwalker.

I wasn't thinking about anything in particular.

I left the Calle 19 de Febrero and the Plaza Mártires del
12 de Abril behind me. Only a few people were strolling
beneath the trees. The smell of fermented pineapple grew
stronger in the evening air, a sign that the following day's
weather would be variable. For the moment, it was hot and
humid, the way it always is in Puesto Libertad. I was thinking
about the heat. And the humidity.

Farther along on the Calle Insurgentes del 28 de Enero,

my head stopped lolling weakly on my chest and started tipping backward. I leaned against the trunk of the nearest palm tree to catch my breath. I watched the clouds, the sky, the giant guandiras flapping in the treetops. It was the hour when they're already busy stretching and exercising their dark brown, leathery wings.

The landscape was sweating profusely. When I stuck out my tongue to lick up a few drops, I found they had a rusty taste.

Hey, come along with me, said a voice in my ear.

Without turning around, I could tell that it was Rui Gutiérrez. I hadn't heard him sneak up to my tree. I looked at him. He was wearing his usual military rags, his marsh commando's outfit. Something in his knapsack recoiled and spat, then twisted slowly, then writhed frantically. Gutiérrez walloped it. He stank of manioc wine, and his gestures seemed exaggerated.

They're breaking you down, he said.

Oh, not too much, I replied. I've been through worse.

I pried myself loose from the trunk of the palm tree. Ants were hard at work between my shoulder blades, toiling over the bloodstain on my shirt. During my little visit to the Auguani kitchen courtyard, I'd been splashed with crocodile. Disturbed at their labors, the frightened ants began to stampede up and down my spine. Gutiérrez, who was not partial to chaos, sent them packing with a deft backhander. Then we left.

Gutiérrez did not reproach me for the imperialist impoverishment of my vocabulary, for the palm tree, the ants, the crocodile any real Indian would naturally have called a jacaré. He'd understood the wretched state I was in, and he possessed a sense of friendly sympathy that must have prompted him to spare me. Still, I should note here that Gutiérrez was a revolutionary to the core, that a sincere internationalism flowed through his veins, and that the essence of internationalism is compassion toward the downtrodden, toward victims and poor bastards of all kinds.

We walked slowly along the Avenida Bandera, that broad street sloping down to the docks and the riverside neighborhood. Vines stretched from branch to branch, blocking the view. We caught no glimpse of the evening light glinting on the Abacau, or the Cocambos' shacks, or the streets leading to the residential district.

Gutiérrez was staggering as badly as I was. He was ill. I could hear his teeth chattering. Malaria never gives us any peace. Gutiérrez had tried in vain to stave off the attack, to forestall the inevitable fever. He had his own remedies, concocted with wine and aromatic plants patiently masticated by some old women, neighbors of his in the slums of Manuela Aratuípe.

What teeth I have left chattered along with his, just to be companionable. Our decrepit constitutions kept each other company.

Have you noticed that pineapple smell?

What? he groaned.

All around us, Puesto Libertad was putting the finishing touches on nightfall. The giant guandiras were already patrolling the darkening heavens. The daytime insects fell silent, giving sudden prominence to the last-minute melodies of the songbirds. Then raucous bands of black monkeys burst on the scene, insolent little saguyanas, real devils, whose obscene grunts instantly destroyed the serenity of the evening.

Don't worry, Golpiez, said Gutiérrez. We're going to escape.

He pointed into the distance, toward utopia and shamanism and primitive camaraderie with outcasts and fringe dwellers, Jabaanas or Cocambos or some even more miserable bunch as yet undiscovered and unrescued. In the patch of sky to which he pointed soared a bat.

And before we go, we'll settle their hash for them, just as sure as I'm standing here.

Now he was pointing lower, toward the trees, toward the saguyanas. The little monkeys found us interesting. They clambered briskly down from the branches. They bounced around in the dust yowling gibberish at us. They galloped along the avenue, drawing closer to us as they frisked about like disjointed puppets, and, screeching constantly, they joined hands to form howling circles, braying chains, advancing cautiously only to retreat in terror, then embellishing this feigned panic, scurrying back up the palm trees to shake the fronds until they rustled harshly. You could see their tiny fangs, their red gums.

Golpiez! they shouted. Gonçalves! Golpiez! Gonçalves!

You hear them? asked Gutiérrez indignantly.

I was not pleased to be thus linked, on a public thoroughfare, to a Jucapira whose name was mud over on the Calle 19 de Febrero.

Lend me your blowpipe, I said.

I'm out of arrows, sighed Gutiérrez.

Fabian-Fabian! chanted the monkeys. Golpiez-Gonçalves!

Don't listen to those little weasels, huffed Gutiérrez. It's all lies. I was never in Mapiaupi during the July massacres.

What? I asked. I was shaken.

They tell the wildest stories, complained Gutiérrez. I was among those troops who entered Mapiaupi, it's true, but I wasn't ever assigned to the execution squads. At least not to the ones shooting people down by the river.

I tried to concentrate on the task at hand: listening closely to the saguyanas' squeals and denunciations, but I didn't catch anything new. Golpiez Fabian! Gonçalves Fabian! And not one syllable more. They had nothing to say about the July massacres.

In any case, at least not in July, insisted Gutiérrez, clinging to my arm.

They're moving off, I observed. They're leaving. Can't make out what they're saying anymore.

I did not want to start delving into the auditory hallucinations of Rui Gutiérrez. All things considered, the shootings at Mapiaupi weren't such a bad memory for me. They'd allowed me to leave the world as a martyr and to escape the long arm of the Bandera at the right moment. I had no desire to explore my executioners' remorse. And no desire to learn their names. Gutiérrez's responsibility in this business left me cold.

I held no grudge against the men who shot me.

The next time, we'll have ammunition, I assured him. Patience, Rui. The next time, we'll stick them full of arrows.

His reddened eyes crinkled with excitement at the prospect of such revenge.

Right, he snorted. We'll show them a good time, just like they showed us . . . That scum . . . Just before we cast off . . . We'll take them as provisions for the journey . . .

We'd reached the Calle Comandantes. Beneath the trees, the light was caught between sunset and moonrise.

Calle Comandantes, I announced. We're two minutes from the Calle Escalante. Want to go see Manda?

Gutiérrez halted. Deep in his knapsack, the thrashing began again. Gutiérrez stifled it. Jaçanarana, he said. Even decapitated, it squirms around for hours.

Want to go see Manda? I repeated.

Not recommended, said Gutiérrez.

Why's that, not recommended?

It's Thursday. She's got company.

No, I said. Days when she works at the oil mill, she doesn't see anyone. She's already told us that a million times.

Golpiez, you're in for a nasty surprise, warned Gutiérrez.

He was having a fit of the shakes. His fever was rising. He uncorked the gourd at his belt and gulped down several mouthfuls of his alcoholic potion. Then we cut across the Calle Comandantes and worked our way down the Calle Escalante, slinking from yard to yard to avoid detection, creeping quietly along as far away from the houses as possible. Gutiérrez had wangled me into that—approaching like an army scout or a burglar. We'd agreed to knock on Manda's door only if she didn't have any visitors.

We used tunnels in the vegetation that Gutiérrez seemed to know backward and forward and with his eyes closed, since he'd already used them so many times in the twilight and evening hours. These thickets were damp with dew. A colony of caranguejeiras escorted us along one twenty-yard stretch. These spiders are very strong, with impressively long legs. The Cocambos claim that they possess remarkable intelligence and are by nature suited to the collective life, and that in certain inaccessible areas of the rain forest they establish utopias more revolutionary and even more successful than our own. The caranguejeiras observed us with their octonocular stare.

At times this carmine gaze glittered in the shadows.

I held my breath from the moment we brushed past the first web.

Without making any fuss, Gutiérrez simply wriggled on through the tangle of plants. Then we tramped along paths frequented by monitor lizards, squashing wild vegetables much appreciated by toads and iguanas. We passed close by the Auguani houses in the Escalante neighborhood. Whenever we sniffed the odor of frying near one of those shacks, we'd hug the muddy ground and rotten leaves even closer. That's how we spent the last few moments of daylight.

Then Gutiérrez stopped wobbling along in front of me. Before us loomed a bulky brown mass, ten or fifteen steps away.

We could hear voices, and sighs.

I recognized the place. We'd come out at the back of Manda's hut. Gutiérrez had just begun croaking in order to cover the noise of our passage across the damp soil, through the grasses and weeds I mentioned before, although their names aren't important: tapirapecús, taramiaranas. Urged silently on by Gutiérrez, I crouched low and waddled off to the left.

Manda's lamp wasn't lit, but inside the hut a whispered conversation was going on, which I could hear more clearly as I moved to the left. I picked my way through clumps of taramiaranas until I could put my ear against the wall and listen, staying perfectly still. It was simple for me to figure out that I was right behind the head of Manda's bed.

The stars came out one by one, then by entire nebulae. The garden was dark. Gutiérrez was croaking. Toads were answering him enthusiastically, without managing, however, to duplicate his rather unctuous glottal stops. I could feel the ground worn smooth under my feet, the nettles trampled down during previous eavesdropping sessions. Someone else had often waited there.

You could hear the fatigue in Manda's voice, a relaxed fatigue, almost serene.

Oh, no, Fabianito, she was saying. It's nothing to be afraid of. It's Golpiez, hunting iguanas.

Manda's visitor moved on the bed—and then his fist hammered the plank right where my cheek was pressed. Through my eardrum came thunder and indignation.

Cut it out, Golpiez! ordered the visitor. No more iguanas! You've eaten enough of that revolting meat! As though there weren't any fruits on the trees!

Don't be angry with him, said Manda.

First big revelation of that December. Gonçalves and

Manda were sleeping together.

Don't be angry, Fabianito, Manda was saying. He's a Jucapira: he eats those things because he's worried they'll accuse him of not being Indian enough.

I'd sat down to one side, in a puddle. I was shaking. My mind was blank and I was shaking.

A little way off, in the darkness, Gutiérrez kept on croaking.

21

THE FOLLOWING day, I was allowed a breather. No
Auguani from the political security unit arrived to drag me
from my hammock at dawn. There were days like that, when
the judge's assessor—who was in charge of the interrogation schedule—preferred to let me marinate and stew and
simmer and go all to pieces on my own, without the technical assistance and helping hands I usually enjoyed in the
kitchen courtyard.

I got up and went to sit on my doorstep. The weather was
cloudy and variable. Passing heavy showers followed by
clearing; low clouds, sultry atmosphere, shifting winds.

Parrots brightened the Calle 30 de Abril from time to
time. I spent the morning thinking about lexicographical
problems. We may harbor the most profound feelings of
loathing and disgust, yet we smother them with appallingly
minor details.

A few names of parrots and their close relatives. Araracã,
arariti, ajurupoca, maracana, maracanã-guassú, maué,
tiriba, cacaué, ajurucuruca, ajururu, ajurujucanga,

araçuaiava, aracanguaba, cuiúba, tuí, baitaca, cuiú-cuiú, tanajuba, sabiaci, yuruquarique, yandaya. Thinking about the birds kept my misery at bay.

Gutiérrez turned up around noon. He was still burning with fever. The jaçanarana in his knapsack was no longer writhing; it now took the form of slices wrapped in banana leaves, already grilled over one of the charcoal fires of Manuela Aratuípe.

We sat down far from the mud puddles and at a distance from the anthills. The orchids overhead were called urucatus, according to Gutiérrez, who despite his trembling had intercepted my questioning glance. We silently ate a few stringy mouthfuls of snake. And then we could no longer postpone our conversation about Gonçalves.

Rather than stir up the memory of the previous evening's expedition and suffer afresh the picture of Gonçalves surucating with Manda, I repeated to Gutiérrez what was written on the brass nameplate by the front door of the dentist's house: Fabian Gonçalves, former chief psychiatrist, Veterans' Hospital of Juaupes; psychologist, Social Services Department of Puesto Libertad.

Social services! Juaupes! sneered Gutiérrez.

He noisily spat out a bit of jaçanarana backbone that was giving him trouble. Flies settled immediately on this gummy treat.

Let me tell you something, said Gutiérrez. He must have been sent to a village in the back of beyond, out in some poisonous old swamp of a jungle. There he was, surrounded by flooded rain forest, by igapos and hanks of hanging moss, and the Indians who came to consult him didn't speak Jucapira, and they wore necklaces of human ivory and pendants made of hair or shriveled sexual trophies pierced by maracana plumes, and all that began to get to him, scared him so much he went crazy. He's a Jucapira, remember, and they just can't take it, drowning in wilderness with no way out. Jucapiras get nervous when they see trees overhead.

Not all of them, I objected.

He ignored my remark. Talking about Gonçalves infuriated him, and this irrational anger—on top of the malaria—would make him rant on all by himself. I tried to look into his eyes: two reddish marbles with hugely dilated pupils. He was off and running. Until he reached the point of hysteria and subsequent collapse, he would only become more and more belligerent.

The Jucapiras can't take it, he insisted. They go berserk. Fear ate away at him day after day, an uncontrollable fear he couldn't admit to anyone without being found out for what he was—not a real Indian, just a tourist, and a traitor. And he abandoned his post during a period of great revolutionary ferment, without any thought of the consequences for the population, and when he got to Puesto Libertad, he hid behind a whole bunch of lies, behind a so-called medical practice at Juaupes, behind a so-called spotless revolutionary career, behind a so-called psychiatric self-abnegation, behind . . .

Gutiérrez stopped. He looked at me, but did not see me. Sweat stood out on his brow and eyelids. He got up, went off to vomit, and returned to sit down again, trembling, his face drawn.

I've got friends among the Auguanis in the political security forces, he said. They're going to discover the truth about his past.

This remark bothered me. I started to defend Gonçalves, which outraged Gutiérrez. He'd taken a wicked-looking machete out of his knapsack; he now examined the stained blade with fastidious care.

That's enough, Golpiez!

He studied me disdainfully. Down at the Calle 19 de

Febrero, they sized me up with that same look of hatred. Now and then the wings of the little blue dragonflies fluttering around us would crackle.

Since you get along so well with him, said Gutiérrez, he must have told you all about his adventures. Juaupes and afterward. Tell me everything. I want to know. So you can go report it all to your Auguani friends? He gestured eloquently with his machete. Tell me everything, from A to Z. Let's go, Golpiez. Spill it before I . . .

I considered an oily stripe on the blade he was brandishing and hesitated no longer. I told the dentist's story just as Gonçalves had related it to me—one of his versions, anyway, because each time he retold it, the specific circumstances and the chronology and even the main events would change.

As often happens when I'm threatened, I was in no hurry to reveal the heart of the matter—supposing such a heart existed and could in fact be revealed.

One fine day, I said, he slipped the key under the hospital door. A haze of stifling humidity lay over the village of Juaupes. The insects' corrosive racket was maddening, and Gonçalves had been enduring it for several years now, from dawn to dusk and then all night long. He panted as though a mob were at his heels. Salty droplets trickled down his dark skin, leaving tracks in the dust. He looked around at the cluster of a dozen communal and individual huts, and at the dogs strewn about the foreground, asleep with their tongues hanging out, done in by ticks and the heat. Off to one side, the clinic looked like a shack that had been abandoned for weeks. The roof was caving in beneath the convulsions of twining or creeping or strangling plants. Gonçalves backed away. Now he was observing the village from a little farther off, in fact he'd had to poke his head between two cascades of flowers to take this last look. They were red blossoms, the ones he'd used to make necklaces whenever there was a feast, magnificent strands of blooms that he offered to the guests, receiving in exchange pendants of jaguara tongues or vulvas, garlands of pink shells, and tatus' tails. A minute later he let this curtain fall, and the hospital disappeared. The first mosquitoes of the journey assembled on his sweaty legs. The noise was deafening: every winged thing was chirring or whirring at top volume. He raised his bush knife and began hacking out a path to the igarapé where his pirogue was waiting.

Perfect, said Gutiérrez. But now skip the details and speed it up.

Gutiérrez swayed in front of me, dripping with perspiration just like Gonçalves, and waving his machete around just like him, too.

I was anxious to see his fever move from the aggressive to the delirious phase, but for the moment I wasn't sure if he was getting ready to vomit or hack open my forehead or perhaps slice through my cheeks.

Sometimes I fight back against degradation, I explained. I force myself to adopt a literary style. I try not to keep cranking out the same phrases.

Cut out the folderol or I'll cut out your heart, said Gutiérrez. Got that?

Got it, I said.

He walked two steps away, vomited, and returned. He was shivering.

I continued.

Going downriver, I said, he runs into an ambush of government soldiers. The 28 de Enero faction or the 30 de Abril dissidents—I don't remember which. He lets himself get recruited, takes part in several campaigns, but after three or four years they accuse him of belonging to the

Bandera and they stick him full of spears, then send him on
back to Juaupes, where he's tried and executed.

He deserved it, grumbled Gutiérrez. The 28 de Enero
faction! The Bandera! A load of crap!

They execute him, I repeated. They finish him off with a
poisoned bullet behind the ear, and they lay his body out in
a canoe.

I went on like that for a few minutes. I grafted onto the
narrative body various items of little or no use to the investigators of the political security forces. I sent my character
drifting along the twists and turns of the Pirauana, on the
igapos and channels and lagoons of a deadly—indeed, a
horribly deadly—region. My audience's attention began to
flag. He was calming down, although he still interjected
spiteful comments here and there. While waving his slaugh-
tering knife around, he'd slashed the palm of his left hand.
Blood dripped onto the spewed-up gobbets of snake lying in
front of him.

The Pirauana! he said disdainfully. And some people
think I'd fall for that!

With melancholy disgust, the two of us watched his blood
soak into the ground.

Continue, Golpiez, he said. Continue. Don't mind me.

So he stayed, lying down without paddling, for weeks and
months, I said, or perhaps years and even longer. You know
how that kind of time cannot be measured. The pirogue
floated at a leisurely pace beneath vaults of vegetation. It followed the black or yellowish meanderings of nameless
rivers, drifting from lake to lake, often losing its way in
labyrinths of painfully dazzling colors, beneath the her-
metic dome of leaves, often brushing past low-hanging
masses of vines. I'll spare you the names of the vines. There
were hundreds of different kinds.

Cut it short, murmured Gutiérrez.

His eyes were closed, and he was shaking with fever. Even without the scars disfiguring his mouth, his face would have been twisted by suffering. His eyeballs were jerking convulsively beneath their twitching lids, and pulsing veins stood out on his neck. The aggressive phase had passed. I went over to him and made him let go of the machete. The messy gash in his left palm had an evil look to it. I cleaned the wound as best I could. He hardly reacted at all. He was babbling.

Don't stop, he said. I'm listening.

His head drooped. While he mumbled and rambled on, I realized that my monologue was now in danger of becoming a soliloquy, and that I would have to ask the questions myself if I wanted to make my answers seem lifelike.

In my story, Gonçalves wandered around the upper reaches of the Abacau for a long time. Then he joined various insurrectional movements once again and fought in this or that rebel army and then he was killed and then he collected material for a dictionary of the common native language and then the Bandera's police sent a burst of gunfire ripping through his chest.

Hurry it up, Golpiez, I told myself periodically.

Move on to the next adventure, I'd advise myself, mimicking Gutiérrez's threatening gestures while Gutiérrez looked on, unseeing.

Then the psychiatrist paddled along, still half asleep, toward Puesto Libertad.

His face had begun to wither and fade, I said. And at the very moment when he finally set foot on the wharf at Puesto Libertad, at the lower end of the Avenida Bandera, his ears fell off and plopped onto the planks, right in front of his sandals, with a noise like the splattering of overripe figs.

The first sign of deafness, I commented, sneering the way Gutiérrez does.

No, I replied. Actually, his hearing loss occurred as a result of the skin graft. Over on the Calle 19 de Febrero, where they'd taken him for the registration formalities—verification of identity, application for a residence permit . . .

We know, Golpiez, I said. Don't waste time on such trivia.

Gonçalves was squatting in the kitchen courtyard, I said, and a sympathetic colleague performed a hurried emergency operation.

What colleague? I scoffed.

Perhaps it was the dentist, I said. He never saw him again. There was a dentist present, over near the infirmary door, between the kitchen and the tortoise pen.

All right, go on, I said.

The dentist sewed them on right there—ears taken from an Indian woman who had just collapsed in front of the pen, a Cocambo who'd succumbed to the livelier aspects of the interrogation.

No Cocambo has ever been mistreated by anyone, I objected. Even the Bandera has always considered them beneath notice. Even the Bandera's police . . .

A Cocambo or a Cayacoe, I said.

When he'd arrive at this point in his adventures, Gonçalves would always describe the tragic beauty of this Indian woman, a Cayacoe who, like all Cayacoe women, resembled Manda, and he would evoke in detail the smell of crocodile's flesh and crocodile's dinner emanating from the greenish pool at the far end of the courtyard, a smell that clung to all the municipal buildings, a smell to which Gonçalves had not yet grown accustomed but which was already poisoning his lungs, and which he already associated with the pernicious nature of Puesto Libertad. The smell of a revolution that had reverted to its primeval inexistence.

And that was that, the psychiatrist would moan. A colleague of questionable competence! You'd have thought he'd sewn the things on with his foot! The stitching was a mess, the sutures on the lobes were crooked . . . My ear canals surrounded by foreign cartilage! It was sheer butchery! You see?

And he'd show me.

I'd lean forward to inspect the cranial landscape, the marks of clumsy sewing, numerous revolting scars. The outer ears themselves possessed an undeniable feminine charm, covered as they were with a downy bloom of a light peach color that one's fingers longed to caress.

Moisture would glisten at the roots of Gonçalves's hair. He was awaiting my verdict.

I can't see a thing, Doctor! I'd cry. Hardly anything! It's invisible!

I interrupted myself.

Gutiérrez was asleep, beyond the reach of my clowning. Dragonflies crackled, hovering before his mouth, before his secret delirium.

The heat had grown more sweltering. Clouds were rapidly turning black; lightning shot through them in a blinding gray flash, but there was no thunder, and not a single treetop rustled.

Come on, let's go, I said. We'll have a drink over in the Cocambo quarter. We're standing up and we're leaving.

Gutiérrez didn't answer.

The dragonflies crackled before his lips, and then came over to click before mine, hovering steadily where my last words had died away.

Hovering over nothing.

22

IN THE hope of escaping further interrogations, Fabian moved several times that month, but in vain. Puesto Libertad is not a place where one can easily disappear. Two Auguani thugs would show up bright and early wherever Fabian had spent the night: in his shack on the Calle 30 de Abril, or in some abandoned hut, or else at Manda's place (despite her liaison with the psychiatrist, Golpiez continued to visit her and surucate with her as though nothing had changed), or somewhere else, under a dock down by the water, for example, or on a pile of sodden leaves over in Manuela Aratuípe, behind Gutiérrez's miserable home, or even in the room of some Cocambo prostitute made oblivious by Indian drugs to both his arrival and his departure.

The Auguani toughs would escort him to their headquarters, where he would wait in the second courtyard until noon, attached to the stake used for skinning monkeys, or left untied, sitting on his heels between the tortoise pen and the jacaré pond, while the assessor checked his dossier and decided which questions required more detailed answers before sunset that day.

Then the inquisitors went after those answers. They would often use against me things that Gonçalves had said or that I had confided to him during my trances or our slide-viewing sessions. In that way, the kitchen staff had found out enough to satisfy them about my dealings with Leonor Nieves.

They had begun concentrating on María Gabriela, the María Gabriela I had known in Mapiaupi, during those years in Mapiaupi when she was the leader of the Bandera (or of the Bandera's police force) and flaunted her intimate relationship with her friend Judge Pomponi. The interrogators tried to prove or make me admit that my somewhat amorous connection with her had never been sincere, and that my sole objective had been to use her to get at Judge Pomponi, to gain his trust and await my chance to assassinate him. This is the kind of logic their questions followed.

Did you surucate?

With whom?

With María Gabriela.

I don't remember anymore. It was so many, many years ago. The memories have faded.

From Yaguatinga you went to Mapiaupi, to find work there as a male nurse.

Yes.

In the psychiatric department of the hospital, there was a female employee named Manda. Did you meet her?

Yes.

Did you surucate with her?

Yes. We lived together.

For how long?

I don't remember now. For months, years.

You traveled from Yaguatinga to Mapiaupi by pirogue. At

dawn, before going in search of such a canoe, you wandered through the deserted streets of Yaguatinga. You found yourself in front of the railroad station, across from the hotel where a Chikraya had been killed during the night. You entered the hotel. Did you notice any traces of this incident?

Out in the patio a Coariguaçu was mending the chicken coop and the cages. There were eight or nine dead hens lying on the ground, a blood-soaked rabbit, several dead guinea pigs. The Coariguaçu didn't say anything. The guerrillas had gathered up the cartridge casings from the automatic weapons and had carried away the Indian woman's body.

Her name?

I don't know.

Leonor Nieves?

I don't know.

Under whose authority had the guerrilla band operated?

Pomponi.

Where did you get this information?

From talking to onlookers hanging around the train station.

So, you remember how many dead hens were lying in the hotel courtyard, but you can't recall whether or not you ever surucated with María Gabriela?

I'm sick. My memory is sick. The psychiatric expert wrote it in my file.

But you can still describe her.

Who?

María Gabriela.

Yes.

Describe her. Your first encounter.

The Astalteca was standing in front of the window, in the rays of the setting sun. I can still see her dark hair and skin and her shapely figure. She heard me approaching and shifted her position slightly. I studied the oval shape of her face, her thick braid of hair, and her black eyes with that glint of green fire that always lends a hint of mystery to the beauty of Astalteca women. She sensed she was being observed. At first a faint exasperation veiled her smile, as if it pained her to endure the looks of admiration and desire directed at her by all men's eyes. But at last she smiled at me. At that time in my life, my appearance was not as repulsive as it is now.

Describe the precise circumstances of this encounter.

The hospital in Mapiaupi. I'd been working there for about ten days. They'd hired me because of my experience as a stretcher bearer in the army. I cleaned up the dying patients, the rooms constantly soiled by the cholera cases. The corridor where this scene took place was in the surgical wing. I'd come there to get three stretchers that were stacked against the wall. You could hear a few patients moaning in their rooms. The doors were closed. Aside from the Astalteca and myself, there was no one.

Explain the presence of María Gabriela in a corridor in the surgical wing.

At that time she was a member of the committee the tribunal had established to interrogate the wounded, the Indian men and women who had survived the attack on the train. Most of the wounded were suffering from gangrene, since they had lain untended out in the open for days alongside the railroad tracks. They'd finally been transported under close guard to Mapiaupi. It was important to question them before they fell silent for good.

Go on with your story.

The Astalteca was wearing a V-necked blouse, cut quite low. I remember the golden bloom of her skin at the neckline. The material was raw silk. She wore a sheath of light-colored leather on her right hip. Dark red skirt, very long, down to her ankles. I bent over to pick up the stretchers.

The Astalteca went back to studying what was going on outside the window: absolutely nothing. Aside from a mangy
dog licking its flanks, the courtyard was empty. Then the
Astalteca entered one of the rooms. I smelled iodine for a
moment, and chloroform.

You didn't try to communicate?

No.

Give a plausible reason.

My mind was on something else. I wanted to remain faithful to the memory of another woman.

Leonor Nieves?

I've forgotten.

Did you ever see María Gabriela again?

Not right away.

Be more precise.

Not for several years.

In the meantime, you work in the hospital at Mapiaupi.
The town is taken and retaken by short-lived internationalist factions, by government troops, by rebel forces. The
medical services barely manage to get by, struggling against
a lack of funds, cuts in water and electricity. From a profes-
sional point of view, you are going nowhere. Making no
attempt to earn further qualifications, you continue day
and night to mop up the sweat and excreta of the dying.
Your efforts to remain at the bottom of the social ladder will
not go unnoticed. You spend much of your spare time with
Manda and a bunch of petty Indian prostitutes, going dancing with them whenever you can, getting drunk in the
Cocambo section of town, even trying sometimes to pass for
a Cocambo, learning their ways and speech habits. You
claim that you agree wholeheartedly with the Cocambo
ideal of nonexistence. You show enthusiasm for guerrilla
initiatives only when large popular demonstrations are
organized in support of them. In any case, the various

revolutionary factions in Mapiaupi leave you alone, possibly because of your social value, which is practically nil, and also perhaps because, at a certain point, you begin to be seen in the company of María Gabriela and Judge Pomponi. This liaison with a couple considered to be among the principal players in the revolution throws your entire dossier into question. Is it true that meetings took place between you and María Gabriela?

Yes.

Did you surucate?

I can't recall. We spent hours together, sometimes with Pomponi, sometimes without him. Harmless chatter, jokes, teasing. She asked me questions about Manda, or about the little Indian whores I knew, or the staff at the hospital, or the wounded who had come into the emergency room. When Pomponi was there, we sometimes told one another our dreams. I dreamed a lot in those years—not as much as the Cocambos, who only really begin to live when they fall asleep, but a lot.

You were more or less the same age as María Gabriela. Judge Pomponi was old enough to be your father. How did you get along?

There was no conflict in our relationship. The judge was a fascinating, seductive person. He made no attempt to hide the attraction he felt for María Gabriela, but at the same time, it didn't bother him in the least when she became temporarily infatuated with someone. He found me harmless and entertaining. He displayed a kind of protective fondness for me, an affection tinged with irony and skepticism. When he felt we needed a change, needed to get out of the city, he'd invite me to go for a walk with him along the railroad tracks that went on to Yaguatinga. We'd tramp through the rain forest together, toward the ponds near Mapiaupi. He would teach me the names of trees.

He taught you their true Indian names, in Auguani.
Jucapiras don't know anything. They start off not knowing
any of the languages of the forest and they wind up confusing them all together. It amused the judge to hear you
babbling in Auguani or the common tongue, under his
tutelage. He had you recite long vocabulary lists. Sometimes
he'd slip in a Sobayaguara word, to see if you'd notice. You
never did. The judge didn't bother to correct you. These
lists were thus engraved in your memory, complete with mistakes. This is why you insist even today on believing that
caranguejeira is an authentic Indian name for that spider.

The Coariguaçus use it, and the Cocambos, and the
Cayacoes.

They use it when they talk to a tourist. When they address
imperialists, assassins . . . Did you kill Pomponi?

No.

You were seen leaving Mapiaupi with Pomponi, on the
path leading to the ponds near the town. Night was falling.
You returned alone. The body was never found, but all
the evidence is against you. Yes or no, did you kill Judge
Pomponi?

I don't remember anymore.

What time was it when you returned from the ponds at
Mapiaupi?

Dawn.

Go on.

The sun was coming up. Just outside the town, I stood
motionless for a moment at the edge of the forest to look at
the clear sky, the majestic trees, the vines. I spent several
minutes naming everything I could. The most common
vines were ibipuyú, cainca, jipioca, urubucaá, and cipotuíra.
Everything gleamed softly, waiting for the sunrise. Frogs
were croaking nearby. When they were quiet for an instant, I
heard twigs snapping in the underbrush. I peered closely at

the green wall forming the edge of the forest. Someone was behind it, spying on me. I saw no one. I walked away.

Did you still have with you the gun you used to shoot Pomponi?

I don't remember.

Did you question Pomponi about the Bandera before executing him?

No.

When did you see María Gabriela again?

After my arrest.

By whom were you arrested?

I don't know. The government troops had just taken over. They were analyzing the situation, gathering information. For the moment there were few casualties. I had arranged to meet María Gabriela in the Cocambo part of town. She had been living in relative secrecy ever since the change of political regime. The sun was really beating down, so I found a patch of shade to sit in. María Gabriela hadn't shown up. I could see the river off in the distance, its flowing waters separated from their banks by treacherous mud flats. The tumbledown houses of the neighborhood gave off dank, musty smells. Then men came and took me away.

Where were you taken?

To a room.

Did you see María Gabriela that day?

The following day. She was a member of the judicial committee that questioned me.

By whose authority was María Gabriela investigating the Pomponi case?

I don't know.

Did you appear before a tribunal set up by the government troops or before the Bandera's police organization?

I don't know. They'd locked me in an empty room. I was handcuffed to a pipe. They never took off the cuffs. I had to lie down or curl up in my own excrement. All I could see through the window was leaves, bushy branches of guaimbira or cumati or quaparaiba. I heard birds outside, and faint sounds of town life. It was one interrogation session after another. At night, they hung a lantern over my head to see me. The electricity was cut off in that neighborhood. In the evening they gave me a little water and some poorly cooked fish. They poured my food out on the ground.

Had María Gabriela ordered that you be given special treatment?

I don't think so.

Was she your principal interrogator?

No. Brief appearances. She supervised.

Describe María Gabriela as she appeared to you then.

I recall that the window was closed and that she would look out through the glass pane, leaning slightly forward, as though she found whatever was happening down there on the sidewalk simply fascinating. I saw her against the light, a three-quarter view, from the back. Her hair was gathered into a thick braid that reached her hips and swung heavily against her back whenever she barked an order at the interrogators or craned her neck to get a closer look at something in the street. I knew the weight, the texture of that hair, because I'd touched it—after all, why shouldn't I say so? I'd caressed it, I'd buried my hands in that hair when it hung loose about her shoulders. I'd often noticed blue reflections in the dense black of her braid, but from where I sat in that room, I saw only a dark mass. Even though dust and weariness had dulled her beauty, I still found her desirable. I remembered our very first encounter, in the hospital corridor. Now, standing at a closed window, she held herself aloof from the sordid reality of the interrogation. She was wearing, as she often did, a pale blouse and a very long skirt. The dominant color of the material was a kind of army

green. Without turning toward either her subordinates or
me, she continued to speak, accompanying each of her
clipped sentences with a subtle and perhaps instinctive
counterpoint of body language, tiny quivering movements
of her torso and thighs. She had always had the same seductive effect on everyone, leaving a lasting and troubling
impression.

You are then freed from your captors by the internationalist troops who take over Mapiaupi.

I'd been hearing shelling for a week, and two days earlier
they'd made a point of telling me that, over in the neighborhood around the hospital, Manda had been shot as a rebel
sympathizer. *Freed*... is not the right term. I was alone in the
room. Some soldiers come in, shoot off the cuff attaching
me to the pipe, but leave the other cuff and dangling bit of
chain still locked around my right wrist. I walk clumsily, so
they prod and push me down the stairs. In the street I'm
shoved into a group of people being herded down toward
the river, toward the Cocambo part of town. I think I catch a
glimpse of María Gabriela in the crowd. Before I can figure
out if she's with the internationalist soldiers or among the
prisoners being driven to their place of execution, I'm hit in
the face with a rifle butt. I think I catch sight of Leonor
Nieves as well, but that's a hallucination that has visited me
almost every day of my life in Mapiaupi, a nostalgic mirage.
I'm hit again with a rifle butt. There are soldiers with
machine guns at every intersection.

While you're walking along, are you thinking about anything in particular?

No.

Be more specific.

I linger over a few memories, thinking of Leonor Nieves,
her voice in the darkness, remembering the black seeds in
her earring.

Does anything of a political nature cross your mind?

I try to imagine what will come afterward, when the revolution will have triumphed or been vanquished and, like us, put to death. I try to imagine what will yet be stirring in the primeval ooze.

And then?

We reach the river bank. They send us floundering out into the mud in little waves of eight or ten people. Then they kill us.

23

DESPITE WHATEVER it may cost me, I must now speak of
the second revelation of that December.

The sun was breaking through the clouds over Manuela
Aratuípe after a passing shower. A thousand reflections
waltzed lazily from puddle to puddle. Gutiérrez was sorting
through a jumbled pile of stuff at his feet, fish hooks and
hooks for catching monitors or snakes. I helped him as best
I could.

Once again I'd led the conversation around to María
Gabriela.

She'd never agree to see me, I said. She's the one who
orders the assessor to open or close an investigation. She's
perfectly aware of the methods used down at headquarters
on the Calle 19 de Febrero—it's unthinkable that she
wouldn't be. If she'd wanted to see that I'd get special treatment from your Auguani friends, she'd have intervened. I
don't have any more illusions about her.

Try someone else, suggested Gutiérrez.

His fever was gone, but his left hand was in a bad way, even though several people had put dressings on the wound: Manda, some old Cocambo women from his neighborhood, a Coariguaçu who worked for the health department. I myself had just applied a plaster of curative gums and resins to his palm, which was swelling and turning livid.

Try Leonor Nieves, said Gutiérrez. I hear you knew her when you were young.

That name always affects me deeply. I tried my best to hide how upset I was.

Leonor Nieves was killed eons ago, I said. It's been thirty years, a whole millennium since she vanished.

Possibly, admitted Gutiérrez. But she's here now, in Puesto Libertad. You ought to ask her for an appointment.

Cut it out, I said.

She's here, he insisted angrily. And she runs the town in accordance with the principles of the Bandera, in secret, with María Gabriela and the other members of the Bandera.

I shrugged. I didn't believe him.

She arrived in early autumn, he continued. I would have told you sooner, and Manda knew it, too, but Gonçalves . . .

What, Gonçalves?

He forbade us to mention it in front of you. He wanted to keep the news from you as long as possible. He was afraid you'd lose your mental equilibrium.

Oh, I whispered. My mental equilibrium.

With my right hand I was mimicking a spider, a sleepy caranguejeira, its legs stirring with an awakening energy that was impossible to fathom. I imitated its closed mind, the weary obstinacy with which it clings to its existence.

This little hand theater—that's one of the few things I can still manage to do.

24

THE WAITING room in the town hall was a long, narrow room furnished with two chairs and a plank laid across a few sawhorses. The receptionist, an unattractive Jurucutu woman, rocked back and forth on one of the chairs, yawning. The guard got up from the other to stretch his legs and lord it over Fabian, who had been squatting over by the wall since early that morning and who was just emerging from his daydreaming, showing signs of life.

No point in fidgeting like that, announced the guard. Stay where you are. They'll call you.

Fabian looked at the worm-eaten staircase behind the receptionist. It led to the floor above, and not a single person had used it during the last three hours.

You're sure you gave them my message? he asked.

The guard turned around without answering and went to drink from the pitcher sitting on the table. Then he returned to loom over Fabian with all his raw Auguani bulk, fattened on crocodile meat since childhood—assuming that childhood really does exist. He was wearing camouflage pants frayed into stiff, dirty tatters below the knee. He was barechested, except for a cartridge belt that had once carried bullets in a distant former life and into which someone, at the beginning of its new career, had stuffed amulets and feathers, but now the leather flapped charmlessly against his sweaty skin. Sitting atop his equally perspiring forehead was some sort of shabby beret.

Who was your message for, again? asked the Auguani. María Gabriela?

No, said Fabian. For Leonor Nieves.

It's the same office, observed the man disdainfully.

He turned on his heels and went to stand in front of the door, where he studied the Plaza Mártires del 12 de Abril and its gardens with their deserted paths, and across the street, Gutiérrez napping under a palm tree. He walked back through the waiting room and sat down across from the Jurucutu, propping his elbows on the table. From time to time, the Indian woman would glance briefly at Fabian. She was truly ugly.

After a moment, the Auguani got up again. He walked around a bit, stepped on a cockroach, finished it off, and went back over to Fabian.

Lunch break, he announced. We'll be closed to the public. You can come back later, or tomorrow, if you like.

I stood up without arguing. As far as the Auguani was concerned, I was already gone, and he turned his gleaming back on me. The receptionist as well made it clear to me that I had just left. She was fascinated by the cockroach cadaver the Auguani was now pushing over toward the wall.

As we had agreed, Gutiérrez was waiting for me on the plaza. He was sitting in the shade. He was busy with more preparations for the voyage, although nothing had been decided yet. With his right hand and his feet he was untangling bits of string, the possible future usefulness of which was a secret known only to him. His left hand took no part in this operation. The infection was gradually spreading up the arm. Gutiérrez had given up applying dressings, and the wound was now enjoying the fresh air, its livid lips turning a bubbly pink every now and then, occasionally frothing with an evil-smelling foam.

Well? Did she see you?

It's their lunch hour. She'll see me later.

Gutiérrez returned to his untangling.

How's your hand?

The skin's getting all crackled. It doesn't hurt. It'll give off a lot more pus and then the swelling will go down.

I helped Gutiérrez sort out a handful of little strings.

She won't see you, he said suddenly. His voice was grave.

You never know, I said. There's still the whole afternoon. I'll be persistent. I'll ensconce myself in a corner of the waiting room and stay there until she sends for me or comes downstairs. She'll have to come down sometime.

You're just kidding yourself, said Gutiérrez. She won't send for you, she won't come down, you won't see her. Face it.

We were sitting side by side as we talked, across from the town hall and other municipal buildings. The Jurucutu woman and four employees from the administrative department walked off toward the kitchen of the political security headquarters. The guard had closed off the entrance to the waiting room with his hammock. The Coariguaçu who worked in the health department walked by and greeted Gutiérrez with a single diphthong. He was off to the Calle 19 de Febrero as well. So there was no one else around.

I suddenly felt like telling Gutiérrez about a dream I'd had the previous evening, but then I changed my mind. I couldn't describe it convincingly. It would have been just dialogue, an interrogation stripped of its picturesque torture. Gutiérrez wouldn't have had the patience to listen to me.

Through the branches of the palm trees we could see the dead windows of the second floor, where the higher-ups hid out: ten rectangles fitted with glass or cardboard or blocked with straw matting and screens of reeds. No one was ever seen in those windows. No one ever looked out of them.

I recalled something Gutiérrez had once said. We knew of the existence of the municipal committee, and information about their influence on various institutions leaked out now and again, revealing their true power in Puesto Libertad. But no one had ever actually seen them entering or leaving the administrative buildings.

Gutiérrez's remark hadn't frightened me at the time, but here, in the torrid stillness of the noonday calm, his words made me quite uneasy.

Let's go, I said.

There's nowhere to go, said Gutiérrez.

25

TOWARD THE end of the afternoon I went to see Gonçalves at his office.

The Auguanis had let him go after two straight days of interrogation.

I needed to tell him what Gutiérrez and I had just decided.

We're leaving the day after tomorrow, I told him. All we have left to do is load up the canoes and go.

I explained our project to him, in its most recent version. We'd be heading for the sources of the Abacau or the Retiete, depending on the configuration of the lakes and igapos encountered on our journey. In any event, we would be heading west by northwest. After three weeks we would surely have found a suitable place for our new village, an egalitarian commune that we would baptize Juaupes, in his honor. We intended to set up a shaman's dispensary to serve the Cocambos and Jabaanas. I would be using diapotherapy to cure or at least relieve our patients' amnesia. Rui Gutiérrez, for his part, would interpret and exorcise the Cocambos' dreams during sessions of group dancing. Gutiérrez also intended to reenlist, as it were, so that he might be responsible for the military and ideological security of the commune. Because it was spoken by the most downtrodden among us, Cocambo would become the official language. If and when the Jabaanas agreed to speak, we would communicate with them in the common tongue. Manda would be in charge of health and sanitation services.

You're taking Manda with you? cried Gonçalves.

He had that haggard look people get when they've spent forty-eight hours up against the palisade of the second courtyard.

Did they interrogate you by the kitchen? I asked.

Yes. They slaughtered an enormous jacaré and a tortoise.

How many inquisitors were there?

I don't remember. They took turns. It was dreadfully hot.

You'd do well to get rid of those images, I advised him. You'd be better off hiding them under words.

What? he yelped nervously. Stop whispering like that, Golpiez! You know that my hearing . . .

No more brooding in silence! I yelled. Shout these things out loud! The kitchens, the brutal sun! The crocodiles hacked to pieces! Scream the blood away! Cleanse yourself completely!

I saw him wince, double over, and retreat into the shadows as though my voice had physically struck him in the stomach. The psychiatrist's office hadn't been cleared out during the past few weeks, since Gonçalves had been so harassed by the political security forces that he hadn't had time to garden or even simply to take a machete to the growth clogging the windows, so the plants had invaded in successive and voracious waves. The vines from the Pasaje 6 de Mayo and those in the office had twined and intertwined with increasing abandon to obscure all angles, digest the original bushes and pots of flowers, and weave a leafy cocoon around everything they found inedible: the chairs, the desk with its open drawers, the collections of slides, the drafts of the dictionary, and the dental chair. We teetered on the very edge of that exuberant avalanche. Feeling around, Gonçalves tried to recognize the space that was growing smaller and smaller behind his back. He located the armrest of the dental chair.

Let's have all of it! I demanded. Everything the interrogators said and did! And your replies!

Enough, Golpiez! he shot back. You don't impress me!

He had stretched out in the dental chair, however. I aimed a hearty blow at the armpiece looming up between us and sent it swinging wildly off to one side, its joints screeching lugubriously, its chrome fittings glinting like silvery moths amid the lush foliage.

But you resisted the effects of this carnage! I trumpeted. Tell me all about your defensive methods, every trick you used! How you fooled them! The false leads, the lies!

The psychiatrist was sweating heavily. He still wore the shirt he'd had on during his interrogation; the stained and even scabby material was sticking to his chest in ugly folds. With one slap I brought the mechanical armpiece with its little wheel and the dangling drill swiveling back before his face. The drill hung there at eye level, bouncing gently. The wheel, the drill.

I can't make out what you're saying, Golpiez! he exclaimed. You know I have a bad ear! It was sewn on crooked by a shady odontologist, and he was half-dead besides!

Drop the song and dance, I said curtly. I've had it with you and your ears! What did you spill in the courtyard? That's what we're interested in here—and nothing else! What did you cough up to survive? Under the Auguani knives?

Staring into the open jaws of the jacaré?

Gonçalves's mouth twisted convulsively.

Pomponi! he shrieked. I served up his murder! I had
nothing else to offer them! The jacaré was writhing and
jerking! They'd forced my head down onto its tongue! I
repeated your every last word to them! The ponds at Mapiaupi, the judge's assassination!

All the details? I whispered. I was devastated.

All of them and more! he crowed triumphantly. The
whole story! Murder in the moonlight! Even the names of
the different grasses in the clearing!

I cursed in Jucapira, then fell silent.

A few crackling and tearing noises within the mass of
vines revealed that we were no longer alone. Sure enough, a
dwarf monkey soon appeared, a most puny and disheveled
specimen that pushed aside the leaves to get a good look at
us. Its malevolent eyes moved from my face to my companion's, to the dental drill hanging from its wheel, to the notes
for the vernacular dictionary, then onto those objects displayed on the wall and not yet sheathed in vegetable
shrouds: ornaments, clusters of feathers, cache-sexes, bat-
tle-axes, magic shields, weapons. Other saguyana monkeys
popped out of the vines in different spots and inspected the
psychiatrist's office in turn. I knew that soon there would be
enough of them to begin squealing in chorus, linking my
name with Gonçalves and lumping me in with him in their
insane slogans. A blowpipe would have come in handy, but
Gonçalves had broken his in October during one of his
slide-projection sessions by pointing someone out too
sharply. And anyway, I had no arrows.

I could hear the psychiatrist's labored breathing.

A libertarian Cocambo commune, he stammered after a
moment. Juaupes. Jabaanas, if you manage to communicate
with them. The clinic. The slides. Manda . . .

Nothing further.

Well, what about the slides? I prompted him.

You're taking the projector and the photographs with you?

Yes. We're requisitioning them.

And the dental chair? he asked softly.

Gutiérrez vetoed that. Too heavy for the canoe.

The psychiatrist approved the decision with a barely audible grunt.

The monkeys were gradually growing bolder. Their hectic screeching welled up from the orchids and burst into bloom.

Do you hear what they're saying, those dirty stinkers? wailed Gonçalves.

No, I said. And you?

I scrounged around and found a tapir-skin bag, into which I shoved the projector. I emptied the contents of two drawers of slides in on top of that. When I opened the third drawer, spiders ran over to show their displeasure. Not very big ones, yanduís, but they're troublesome, and there were lots of them. Beneath their webs lay extracts from the dictionary. I left this wisdom forever in their watchful care and turned toward Gonçalves.

He was muttering something.

What? I shouted. I can't hear a thing when you mumble! Don't let the monkeys drown you out! Speak up!

Take me with you! he howled. I know how to paddle!

The saguyanas capered all around us, chanting the first names we shared and our last names with their identical endings.

What did you say? I shouted back.

Take me with you! Tomorrow or the day after, it doesn't matter! I'll meet you at the wharf! At the old dock in the Cocambo quarter! Count me in—I'm with you!

26

AT FIVE in the afternoon I went around to the Calle Escalante. It was the day before, or the day after, depending on how you look at it.

Puesto Libertad was still in the background.

Not for much longer, I thought.

The town was streaming with rain.

To avoid arousing suspicions, Manda had worked all day in the municipal oil mill. When I opened her door, she was dabbing scent on her throat and breasts, a cinnamony perfume I liked very much. I hugged her close. Factory smells still clung to her hair: coconuts mashed to a pulp, musty presses, cunduru-wood tubs, bitter fumes. My hair was soaking wet. The nooks and corners of the room gave off a warm vapor; the floor boards were sweating beneath our feet. I felt like surucating standing up. We made some progress in that direction and then gave it up. After a minute we sat down on the edge of the bed. Rain pattered overhead. Then it stopped. Rivulets gurgled outside the hut. Half undressed, Manda pulled away from me.

You stole his projector, she said. He cherished it like the apple of his eye.

The last time I saw him, he was alive and well in his dental chair. He denounced me over at the Calle 19 de Febrero. I might have cut his throat as a farewell gesture.

Sometimes you talk like a bloodthirsty fool, Fabianito.

Aren't we all? I sighed.

Then we discussed our imminent departure.

You've packed your things? I asked.

Two lamps, some cans of oil. A square of cloth. Some healing lotions for Gutiérrez. Everything will fit into a basket.

Since you mention it, did you get a look at Gutiérrez's hand?

Gonçalves says he'll have to have the arm off at the shoulder.

Oh, him, I grumbled. What he says . . .

I tipped Manda backward across the mattress and we launched into the beginnings of some serious fooling around, but the idea of amputation came between us and got somewhat in the way. Nothing really lascivious happened.

Well, I'm off to see Gutiérrez, I said.

I kissed Manda and set out for the Embarcadero Fusilados del 31 de Agosto. I was curious to see what state the Abacau was in and the extent of the mud flats near the river bank. I strolled by the shipyard, past the collapsed piers and other ruins. Walking casually along, I headed for Manuela Aratuípe. The dugout canoes were moored where Gutiérrez had said he would hide them, camouflaged under the pilings of a large shack on a pier at the edge of the slums. No wavelets came curling softly against the hulls. The water stagnated in vast puddles surrounded by putrid silt. The Abacau itself lay a good distance from its banks, off where one could just spot a hint of rippling movement and the first patch of yellow reflections. Farther on, the river flowed more forcefully, sweeping along white flowers, knotted roots, orchids, branches of ibapomonga covered with viscous fruits. The sky was once again azure, and once again resplendent.

The shantytown was still sodden with rain. As I was crossing a shallow little pond, some mud eels wriggled about my ankles. I tried to catch one of them for supper. I skidded around for quite a while, making plopping noises like boiling porridge. My prey escaped.

Walking on the path leading to Gutiérrez's hut, I passed an Auguani going in the other direction; he had taken part in a few of my interrogations, and his specialty was chopping apart the carapaces of tortoises while suspects watched. The tortoise is turned over onto its back, and when it withdraws into its shell, the plastron is hacked open interminably, split again and again as though by a sotted, clumsy, but stubborn woodcutter, drunk on blood and death.

When I see the kind of company you keep, I told Gutiérrez, I begin to wonder what's going to happen to us tomorrow.

Go ahead and wonder, he said angrily. If I hadn't warned that guy, they would have shot us down like dogs tomorrow. Leaving the territory illegally, infringement of harbor regulations, criminal trespass against the fleet, and I don't know what else. We'd never even have made it into the canoes.

And now we will? I inquired.

Gutiérrez turned stubborn. He was scowling, looking around for something to drink.

Did you tell him where we were going? I asked in alarm.

Gutiérrez continued shifting around empty jugs and the gourds containing his decanting and aging wines and pharmaceutical liquors. His face was the picture of gloom. I asked him a few more questions about his talks with the political security forces and his Auguani friend from the Calle 19 de Febrero, but he made no reply. Then I spoke to him about his hand.

Gonçalves came by to check on me, he said.

Late in the morning, the shaman-doctor had examined the wound. He had not minced words in his diagnosis. A form of equatorial gangrene had begun to eat away the fingers and palm from within, and the infection was working its way up toward the elbow; suspicious spots had already broken out on the arm. Without someone to amputate the unsalvable extremities properly, the expedition risked ending in disaster and great suffering. Gonçalves, whose skills in emergency surgery had not been fully appreciated heretofore, proposed as a bonus his psychiatric savoir faire, since the patient would experience serious feelings of misery after the loss of the prehensile organ on his left side. Gonçalves promised morale-healing sessions, magic-lantern entertainments with pictures, simulated interrogations, memorial excavations, antiasthenic reconstitutions—full *son et lumière.*

If I understand correctly, he's coming with us? I asked.

He wouldn't be in the way, observed Gutiérrez. He knows how to paddle.

Gutiérrez polished off the dregs of a few jugs, and then we drank to the health of his still-sound limbs, and then we toasted the inevitable amputation of the unsound bits.

We were soused.

The afternoon was almost over.

Then somehow we began talking about the Bandera. We'd been rambling on, discussing numerous original topics, and suddenly—nothing but the Bandera, the men and women of the Bandera, their barely discernible omnipresence, their modest or cynical selflessness, their adherence to all parties, all factions (even if said factions were mortal enemies and bent on destroying one another), their support of all the variants of revolution, even when the revolution was clandestine or comatose or long since degenerate or inexistent beneath the primeval ooze of inexistence. We didn't understand the aims of these men and women.

It's because we lack an overall view of things, I said.

You always find excuses for them, fumed Gutiérrez. You're always defending them. Your María Gabriela, your Leonor Nieves . . .

Leave Leonor Nieves out of this, Rui, I warned him.

She belongs to the Bandera, he muttered. She shares an office with María Gabriela and carries out exactly the same duties—keeps an inquisitorial eye on every last cog in the machinery, has veto power over the slightest political or technical initiatives of the municipal government, spends her nights going over dossiers. Together they supervise and direct and stay out of sight. They're in seclusion, day and night, up on the second floor. You'll admit that to someone who hasn't known them personally, it amounts to the same thing.

And leave my private life out of this, too, I snapped.

Later, after some new antidepressant libations, we went into town, intending to get to the bottom of these puzzles.

No surprises along the way.

The ground felt springy from the recent storm.

Calle Manuela Aratuípe; a few drops falling now and then from some corolla concealed by the foliage.

Calle Columnas Internacionalistas del 8 de Diciembre. Pasaje 9 de Julio.

When we arrived at the Plaza Mártires del 12 de Abril, within sight of our goal, we became more subdued.

There wasn't a living soul downtown near the municipal buildings.

Our objective: to slip behind the town hall and climb up into a tree before darkness fell, so that we'd have a level or a bird's-eye view of the second floor. Our plan: to observe from our perch what went on inside the offices of the local council, and most particularly inside the office constantly occupied by María Gabriela and Leonor Nieves. We wanted to confirm the physical existence of the two women and try to grasp some element of their intentions, their secret projects.

The Plaza Mártires del 12 de Abril might have been a deserted village square. The evening birds swooped low over our heads. Their wings made no sound in the silence.

The entrance was padlocked. Nothing moved behind the windows of the first or second floors. We went around the corner of the building and followed the blind wall that runs along a section of the Bulevar Insurrección del 28 de Enero, until we came to the forest that cuts off the boulevard. Beyond the blocks of administrative buildings, Puesto Libertad simply ends. There is nothing resembling inhabited or inhabitable territory. Nothing but dense and brutal jungle. Pure, virgin caacangaba, said Gutiérrez, pointing at it with his sound arm, wild caaeté, untamed caaguaçú, and nothing else.

Daylight was fading.

We plunged into the undergrowth, and after proceeding about forty yards thus concealed, had almost reached our target. The edge of the forest came right up to the back of the building housing the most important of the municipal institutions. Branches overhung the roofs; vines nudged the walls and grazed the black openings among their bricks.

Gutiérrez began to scale a ladder of aerial roots. His left arm was giving him trouble. After he'd climbed about three feet he slipped, twisting noisily as he fell, and wound up hanging by his right sleeve among the leaves, which were taking on patches of colorless velvet and losing all nuance to the encroaching darkness. So there he was, swinging gently, like a pensive monkey in battle dress.

Don't worry, Rui, I whispered. Let me handle it.

When he'd gotten back on the ground, I helped him sit down in the tall grasses, steering him away from the local anthills. Grabbing some vines looping down near us, I hoisted myself up to a horizontal branch. The tree was a kind of monster, a jaramataia, around which twined an embiriba, holding on with all its horrid fluffy fibers. Still, I was crawling on something massive and solid.

Gutiérrez was guiding me.

You're at the right height, he announced softly. The office is across from you. Take a quick look and hurry down.

I told him to be quiet. He was distracting me. My reflexes are lousy at that hour, my eyes are tired, my sense of balance is wobbly. It's a time of day when I hate to be up a tree.

You're just in front of the best window, Gutiérrez whispered. Can you make out anything? Do you see them?

Shut up! I grunted.

If I had stretched out my hand at that moment instead of clinging to the tree, I would have touched the mossy or pitted surfaces of flaking bricks. The window was an opening reduced to its most elementary expression, a rectangular hole without either shutters or panes of glass. The office thus communicated directly with the outside. Nothing protected it from whatever might slither or flutter or swoop in—rain, animals, miasmal vapors drifting on the night air. Although the light was quite dim, the office was clearly visible: a large, square room giving off a strong odor of mildew.

There were empty bookcases, an equally empty cupboard, broken and lying on its side, and three chairs sitting strangely close to the door, as though showing that it should not be used, or at least hampering any intruder trying to enter from the hall. Except for the ceiling and the top of the walls, everything was plastered with excrement. The floor, the dead leaves blown by the wind into the corners, the shelves bare of archives—all encrusted with black guano.

Two of the chairs were occupied by very dark silhouettes, almost human in size. These shapes were huddled rather than sitting.

You could at least tell me if you see anything alive in there, anything moving around, whispered Gutiérrez.

Quiet! I begged him.

I couldn't understand what my eyes had discovered, what they were still discovering. A few seconds went by. This scene was under my very nose and I was staring impassively, incapable of thinking or speaking. One of the forms had quivered. It opened and extended the tip of a membranous wing; then, as though threatened by a last trace of daylight, it reenveloped itself in its own leather. The other form hissed. I was taking all this in, but my mind was going in circles, clumsily returning to the same not very illuminating idea. Bats, I kept thinking, hang upside down somewhere, they don't squat awkwardly on chairs. Even giant bats. Even giant guandiras.

Gutiérrez shook some vines dangling from the branches to remind me that he was waiting below.

The first shape stretched again, and to keep its balance, thrust out its chest and an indistinct mass that must have been its muzzle.

The chair creaked.

The twilight was almost gone. There was no reason to linger.

I studied the occupants of the second floor one last time. Suddenly I noticed something. At first I wasn't sure I'd really seen it, in the darkness. I concentrated my attention on that single point. Then I was certain. At the back of the indistinct mass was an ear ornament: three black seeds pierced by a stone needle. A Chikraya ornament, jewelry for a young Chikraya woman. Not for a guandira. Not even a giant one.

Third revelation of December.

And I don't know what I would have made of it in circumstances more favorable to the expression of ideas, in another life, for example, at an imaginary time when neither the revolution nor Leonor Nieves would have degenerated into death or even worse. I only know, through some vague intuition, that I was involved in it. As a witness, or as an accomplice—I was involved in it. So much for the crude realization that stirred in me at this sight.

So, are they there? asked Gutiérrez softly, down in the tall grass.

He shook the vines again and again to make me answer.

I hardly heard him.

My mind was blank.

III
MUD DANCE

27

THE MOMENT I left the Embarcadero Fusilados del 31 de
Agosto and began walking through the reeds, and again
when I began slogging across the colorless muck, I heard an
unpleasant inner voice murmuring that the expedition
would run into trouble. I rejoined Gutiérrez, and my appre-
hension grew. The smell of leeches given off by the pirogues
must have gotten on my nerves, or perhaps it was the sticki-
ness of the night air, or the silence. Hard to say.

I walked ankle-deep in tepid mud.

Gutiérrez was floundering around beneath the ruins of a
shack built over the water's edge, on a pier on the outskirts
of Manuela Aratuípe. That was where he had hidden the
canoes. His left arm hung limp, banging into the pilings,
the dangling remains of the floor, and every single piece of
wood lurking in the shadows. I went over to splash around
as well, staggering about in water up to my knees and crash-
ing into things along with him. We were trying to remove
banana leaves that had been camouflaging the canoes.

We couldn't see much. We'd all agreed to meet an hour

before dawn. Gutiérrez was gasping and trembling. Every once in a while I could smell his breath, which had a fetid odor fairly symptomatic of gangrenous fever in someone already suffering from malaria. Instead of words, his delirium would draw the occasional moan from him. He wouldn't answer questions. When he spoke it was mostly to request that I shut up. He was confusing me with someone else, with Fabian Golpiez, the mentally deceased Jucapira, my schizophrenic patient who was faking being a faker. Gutiérrez kept calling me Golpiez, which made conversation difficult.

Gutiérrez was trying to clean up our seats in the canoe. Smallish shadows skittered away. I made out some spiders, nonvenomous snakes, two rats. Gutiérrez felt around with his good hand and muttered the names of the intruders, as though reciting a curse in Coariguaçu. This did not lighten the atmosphere.

Stop your grumbling, Rui, I said.

He pretended not to have heard me, but quieted down after a moment. The vermin had all been cleared out of the canoe, which still smelled like leeches, but at least it felt clean. Now all we had to do was stow our belongings away in an organized fashion. Hammocks, twine, arrows, blowpipes, iguana hooks, coconuts, five jugs donated by the Cocambos. I won't run down the whole list. Manda was supposed to bring a two-days' supply of food. The other one, Manda's little friend, the lunatic, was responsible for the psychiatric equipment, the slides and the projector he had stolen from me by threats.

They're late, I remarked.

Here they are, announced Gutiérrez.

Now I saw them strolling arm in arm along the Embarcadero Fusilados del 31 de Agosto, each carrying a single bag. I could tell from their nonchalant attitude that they'd

spent the night together and had surucated. It made me
feel sick. Their relationship had always disgusted me, that
strictly animal tenderness between them that lasted and
lasted, despite betrayals and deaths.

That capacity for mutual consolation.

Gutiérrez looked up and watched them arrive as well, a
scowl of hatred on his face.

Sometimes, Golpiez, he said, I wonder why we've saddled
ourselves with this psychiatrist, and that nurse.

We could still leave without them, I suggested.

Gutiérrez scolded me. Promises, word of honor, revolutionary solidarity, memories. I was always talking treachery,
he fumed. Jucapiras talked nothing but treachery.

At least they aren't in filthy cahoots with certain Auguanis
over on the Calle 19 de Febrero, I pointed out.

I wouldn't talk about sleazy connections if I were you,
Golpiez! he shot back. I'd never get involved in an unnatural liaison with those bats in the Bandera!

I wouldn't either!

And last night? he sneered. His shoulders shook with
fever.

I don't know what you're getting at! I exclaimed.

Don't argue so loudly, whispered Manda from above us.
The whole neighborhood can hear you. You'll alert a patrol!

Golpiez was standing near the reeds, silently studying the
sky and whatever he could deduce from it. Myriad stars twin-
kled in glistening streams running north to south over the
Abacau and the virgin rain forest.

Let's hurry up, urged Gutiérrez.

Golpiez stepped into the muck and bent over the second
canoe. Manda helped him bail it out. Evicted spiders landed
on the slate blue mud, immobile, as though stunned by
their sudden deportation.

Then Manda cried out.

A reptile had bitten her and darted away. She shook her hand sharply, wailing in a low voice. The echoes beneath the ruined house had a particularly hollow sound. Gutiérrez offered words of comfort. If we had to have two amputations, then we'd do them: her right hand and his left arm. I went over to examine the bite, which seemed harmless, in the dark. Manda had been bitten on the thumb. I enlarged the wound by cutting a cross in it with a machete; then I sucked out the venom and tried to spit it all over the catatonic spiders sprinkled around us on the slime. I sent Golpiez over to the riverbank to pick some tacumburi or sacaca leaves. He searched through the bushes for a long time. When he returned, I made a dressing for Manda's thumb with the pinguajarana he'd brought back, which is also good for bites, and I put a clean bandage around Gutiérrez's hand.

The four of us were in a bad way, covered with sweat and mire, and the stars were going out one by one while we hadn't budged an inch from Puesto Libertad. We'd finished our preparations, however, and we climbed into the canoes, Gutiérrez with me and Manda with Golpiez.

It had rained the week before, but not enough to flood the ugly mud flats that appear along the banks of the Abacau in that season. The water was too shallow where we were, so the canoes were stuck in the mud. Not even frenzied paddling could shift them. After a splattering minute of going nowhere, I decided to try something else.

Stepping from the canoe, I found the going wickedly slippery. Squelching noises burbled in the darkness. I pushed, I pulled, I felt clusters of bubbles climb slowly and stickily up my legs. The canoe left its smelly, gluey bed with regret and took every opportunity to snuggle back into it, while I cursed to see still overhead the caved-in floor of the collapsed house, the wooden sky of loose debris that persisted in blocking out the real one.

We weren't going very fast.

Gutiérrez held his paddle as best he could, thrashing away with one arm, producing little more than great sprays of black water. Behind us, Golpiez had followed my example and was noisily plodding or kneeling or skidding alongside their canoe.

For eight or ten sputtering minutes, there was intense wheezing and splashing.

Just above the treetops, the horizon had paled to blue gray.

Then Manda started, and let out a moan. She'd been bitten again.

She's beginning to get on my . . . hissed Gutiérrez.

It wasn't a snake, exclaimed Golpiez. It's an arrow!

I listened. My hearing was damaged in the course of some anthropometric formalities at the Calle 19 de Febrero— there was a slight hitch in the verification of my identity— but now I could suddenly hear with crisp clarity the shrill whirring of arrows. I turned around. Gutiérrez and I had rounded the last piling. We were about twenty yards from dry land, perhaps a bit more, but we were still staggering along in shallow water.

Golpiez hadn't gotten very far from the bank. He was up to his thighs in soupy slop, and he was panicking.

They'll get us all! he hollered. Like at Mapiaupi! Summary liquidation! Old memories! The troops, the hail of bullets! By little groups of four! . . .

Men from the political security forces were indeed on the Embarcadero Fusilados del 31 de Agosto, their presence divined and reconstructed sight unseen in the early dawn, six or seven phantoms of more or less the same substance that darkens the night, only perhaps a touch denser. They weren't running around, just standing beyond the reeds and calmly raising long brown blowpipes to their lips. They limited their attack to this shooting of arrows.

We might have known! yelled the psychopath. The internationalist brigades! Gutiérrez's pals! Failure to observe the river regulations! Theft of municipal property! Sinister designs on the fleet!

Shut up, Golpiez! I shouted.

He did.

The Auguanis ashore showed that they had no intention of pursuing us. They were obviously trying to frighten us before letting us leave. In any case, arrows rained down on us. Some landed next to me, striking the hammocks and Gutiérrez's pack. Golpiez was hit in the back, at the base of his neck, in the backs of his arms. Manda was riddled with darts as well. Whenever she was hit, she panted rapidly the way she did when surucating, with little sighs, stifled yelps like the ones she made when we surucated in her shack on the Calle Escalante.

I was still bent double, straining against the right side of the canoe and guided by Gutiérrez, who claimed to have spotted a channel where we'd finally be able to float free of the mud and move quickly out of reach.

We were drawing farther and farther away from the other canoe.

Golpiez and Manda had chosen to go downstream, toward the Cocambo section of town. They were searching for a channel, too. While I struggled with the canoe, I watched them go from one misfortune to another. Day was dawning. Golpiez and Manda got bogged down behind us, to our right, and then farther away, toward the middle of the wharf. They strayed into a mud flat full of tortoise holes. Their canoe was still grounded in muck, but Golpiez had sunk in up to his waist. Manda climbed out of the canoe and back in again. To go around the tortoise holes they'd had to draw nearer the wharf. They were moving away from us, get-

ting smaller. You'd have thought they were determined to
stay within range and that their goal was to reach the
Cocambo dock and be captured. They were moving parallel
to the shore. The Auguanis were slowly keeping pace with
them, harrying them along.

We made it, announced Gutiérrez.

We had reached the channel. The dugout lifted off the
bottom and floated free. I hoisted myself over the side, dripping wet.

We'll head for the little islands, said Gutiérrez.

He went through contortions to paddle without using his
left arm. I helped him out by sculling or paddling, as
needed.

We skimmed over very smooth ink.

When we reached the islets that lie across from Manuela
Aratuípe, we stopped.

Day was breaking in a swirl of riverine odors. Flamingos
watched us from a sand bank, pale pink and one-legged.

Directly across from us, the shantytown was still asleep. We
peered intently at what was happening near the Cocambo
district. The Auguanis had taken up positions on the abandoned landing stage. Golpiez and Manda were still wallowing in the mud. Sometimes they ducked behind reeds to
hide from the arrows. Now and then Manda would get out of
the canoe to lighten it and help Golpiez drag it along.

What the hell are those two doing? said Gutiérrez
impatiently.

He'd just removed from his shoulder a dart decorated
with a tuft of hummingbird feathers.

Wait, I said, don't throw it away.

I'd been hit above the elbow and near the ear. We examined the arrows, sniffing and licking them. Guaipá thorns,
hard as iron, not smeared with any poison.

The other canoe was on the move at last. Manda was

paddling in the bow, while Golpiez had just clambered into the stern. They'd finally found deeper water. At first their uncoordinated efforts spun the pirogue around three times in front of the wharf and the Auguanis and the Auguani blowpipes. Then they straightened out and headed toward us.

They slipped past the pink flamingos and stopped alongside us.

I helped pull out the darts bristling all over them.

Poisoned? asked Gutiérrez.

Manda sat silently in a state of shock.

Not too much, I replied. You'll feel a bit sleepy in the midday heat.

We'll stop to rest, said Gutiérrez.

Shaken by a fresh fit of trembling, he mumbled something unintelligible, instructions for the journey, perhaps, and then he leaned out over the water and vomited.

The flamingos flew off.

A hundred yards away, the shacks of Manuela Aratuípe were awakening. Parrots had begun squawking in Puesto Libertad. Our assailants disappeared up the Avenida Bandera toward their headquarters. A monkey danced out onto the Cocambos's dock and abruptly froze. It wasn't looking at us. It was peeing.

The hardest part of our journey was over: leaving.

After we'd paddled for half a day, the Abacau began to split into numerous branches and swampy subbranches and lakes, a series of lakes that were often simple pools encircled by green cliffs. The foliage went on forever, always in the same vein. Sometimes dark green higher up, light green below. Sometimes the reverse. The water was a reluctant mirror, tarnished with dirty streaks.

Late that morning, monkeys began their capering in what had been the peaceful forest canopy.

Gutiérrez muttered the names of the monkeys. Saitaia, the spider monkey muriqui, saiburí, guigó, coata, caiarara, the golden-pawed caipuyu. A yurupara, which is usually nocturnal, hung from a low vine a yard away and stretched out toward us, as if to touch Gutiérrez's head, as if it wanted to test his reality, thus revealing that it had never seen an Indian face in those parts, or at least not one distorted by pain and delirium. There were also saguijubas and atamaris.

Gutiérrez spoke without an audience, reciting long lists to himself, sometimes breaking off hesitantly for a half an hour or more, as though conscious of the futility of all speech. I compared his lists to what I remembered from the dentist's dictionary, without catching any errors. I could see fever sweat on Gutiérrez's scalp and dripping from his hair. There wasn't a dry spot on his shirt. His left arm moved rhythmically. He'd managed to tie it to the paddle and thus disguise his infirmity.

The tranquil, relaxing sound of steady splashing.

Tangles of snakes around the edges of water-logged old stumps.

Glimpses of sky through the sprays and garlands of orchids.

The two of us would stop, and when Manda and Golpiez had caught up with us, we'd set out again.

The entrance to a channel guarded by two jacaré snouts, which sank without a ripple at our approach.

We proceeded in this impressionistic way, and we lost our way. Now boughs intertwined so low overhead that we had to bend over to avoid brushing against aerial roots or their resident snakes. The sky had turned yellow; it looked like rain. We frequently ran into choking fog. A big cat roared near the bank, a jaguara. A single roar; then silence. The other animals were quiet.

Wait, Rui, I said. I haven't seen them for a while.

He stopped paddling, hunched over, and collapsed without a word.

Manda and the madman had been following us, often lagging behind or dropping out of sight. We'd managed not to become hopelessly separated.

When Manda emerged from the mist she was almost unrecognizable. Her eyes had lost their sparkle; the Cayacoe features in that kind and obliging face were now stamped with death. I remembered Manda's humble beauty, the spontaneous way she had of sharing its remnants among Gutiérrez, Golpiez, and myself. I recalled her detached observations and sound judgment, her indifference to the world, and the way she had consoled me when I emerged shattered from that place on the Calle 19 de Febrero.

Fabian Golpiez sat quaking in the stern, also ravaged by the toxic sap of the guaipá thorns, or by a new bout of malaria.

Their canoe came up alongside ours. It reeked of male and female sweat, clotted blood, mud. The smell of male and female disaster. Gutiérrez caught a whiff, sat up again, and gave us all a worried look. Then he vomited.

A good time to question him.

You're sure we're going in the right direction? I asked.

No, he replied, growling something else no one could quite make out.

We could stop at a Cocambo village, I suggested.

You know of any Cocambo villages around here, Golpiez? he answered testily.

Manda had closed her eyes.

They're a long way off, she said.

We're already within sight of the river's source, babbled Golpiez, shutting his eyes as well. We can see the lake, the beginning and the end. It will soon be dawn. Day will break all across the horizon, from east to west. Herons, barely visible in the half-light, will skim over the waves. And flamingos, and cranes. The canoe will rock beneath me like a cradle. I will feel no fear. Then suddenly the Cobra Grande will rise into the air, the Mother-of-all-waters will come toward me, breasting the masses of floating leaves, and . . .

Stop it! I yelped. That hokum for tourists! Those dried-out, dusty dreams! Give us something else, can't you?

Don't listen to him, Fabianito, said Manda.

I scowled. I didn't know which one of us Manda meant.

A few drops of rain pattered down.

Let's get under cover, said Gutiérrez. We're all dead tired. We'll set up camp and stay here overnight.

We got Manda out of the canoe and helped her stagger over to a tree, where we sat her down. She was breathless, unable to hold up her head. Her dress was covered with slime and stank of decay.

I squatted down beside her. The darts had pierced her more or less all over, and the wounds were now little swollen craters that looked hard or pulpy, depending on their location. Her arterial pulse was distressingly uneven. Her body had absorbed too many toxins. I undid the dressing I'd applied to the snake bite she'd received that morning. The wound had begun bleeding again. I washed it with rain water and urine, then wrapped it in fresh grasses.

The storm had broken out. Gutiérrez and Golpiez were erecting a temporary shelter with branches. After the first chilly minute, the rain felt boiling hot. Lightning flashed close by three times. To speed up construction of the hut, I left Manda and tackled the nearest banana tree with my bush knife. We were all shivering more and more violently. We were struggling the way one always does when camping, in a running—and losing—battle with water. Cataracts crashed down on the forest, the river, and our skulls.

Manda collapsed. I saw her lying on her side in the grass. Her dress was open, exposing her impressive breasts to the rain.

Four yards away from our shelter, the canoes were filling rapidly. We pulled them ashore and turned them over. While Gutiérrez secured our most precious belongings by tying them to branches, Golpiez drew Manda's dress across her breasts and carried her beneath the roof of leaves. Then Gutiérrez went all around the clearing to chase away any reptiles, killing one with his machete, a two-headed moyacica. I don't eat snake, but Gutiérrez and Golpiez were delighted with the catch. Blood dripped from Gutiérrez's knife.

We sat in our shelter, with the hostile forest at our backs. Eventually Gutiérrez went into his mumbling routine again, cataloging the palm leaves in the roof and then naming all the palm trees in general, whether they were present overhead or not. The puruma, he muttered, the ucuriaguaçú, the jassytara, the putauá, the açai, the fruit of which may be squeezed to produce a refreshing drink, at least when it can be served fresh, which means never, and the batantám with its hard-shelled nuts, the mucumucu, the jiriba, the uricuri, another coconut palm, the bubunha, another coconut palm, the bataiporam—which is really a small butia, the caiané, the babaçu, another coconut palm, the fiendishly spiny geriba, the indaiá, the mucajá, the jarina, which produces very tough black seeds.

Yes, said Golpiez. Chikrayas use them for ear ornaments.

And not only Chikrayas, cackled Gutiérrez, looking over at me. Giant guandiras have ears, too.

Be quiet, murmured Manda. You're beating me over the head with nonsense while I lie here dying.

I'm here, I said. I won't abandon you, Manda.

You've abandoned me so often, Fabianito, moaned Manda.

That's because they kept tearing me away from you to kill me, said Golpiez. They dragged me away, far from the revolution, and handcuffed me to a pipe in an empty room. They questioned and questioned me relentlessly, leaving me to rot in my own piss and shit. Then others took over. They brought me to the river bank, in front of the Cocambos' filthy shacks, and they made me go down into the mud, and walk backward, away from them. Then they shot me.

That was in July, said Gutiérrez. I wasn't assigned to the firing squads that month. Not once.

Nobody's blaming you for anything, Rui, said Golpiez.

For an hour or two, we watched the rain pelting down into the river. Each of us alternated between periods of raving volubly in a low voice and phases of complete stupor.

Golpiez repeated his story of the empty room several times. His descriptions of it swarmed with details. In contrast, he never said anything specific about the interrogation or the interrogators.

They didn't stick you in there just for the hell of it, observed Gutiérrez at last.

The Pomponi affair, I said.

Golpiez gave a little shrug, feigning ignorance.

Stop evading the issue, Golpiez! I said menacingly. Rake up those memories! Skip the decor! Give us the facts!

I took down one of the bags hanging from various branches and unpacked the projector, along with three handfuls of slides that were being—had been—ruined by the humidity.

Pomponi! I exclaimed triumphantly. The judge! The image of the father! The learned rival, the one who initiates, the one who knows!

Gutiérrez helped me set things up. He tipped a jar of

coconut oil over the reservoir in the lamp. There was something ugly in his smile.

The one you kill! I cried.

The storm raged on.

It was the final session with Golpiez. We all felt this intuitively and would never have used the foul weather as an excuse to cancel or delay or shorten this last in the series.

So the investigation took place amid the downpour, the mist, and the earthy smells of the forest floor. A leaden half-light allowed the slides to glimmer legibly against a screen of dense undergrowth. We were frequently blinded by lightning. The atmosphere was uncomfortably close, and we were packed into the tiny hut, but we shivered constantly, without noticing it, in our own personal rhythms.

Golpiez and I were the only ones talking. Manda and Gutiérrez dozed. A word would occasionally bubble up from their unconscious minds, only to degenerate into something unintelligible.

It's nighttime, Golpiez, I said. Your walk with Pomponi outside of town.

My stock of images was composed of two distinct groups that alternated at random. First series: Mapiaupi and its surroundings. Second series: the Calle 19 de Febrero, headquarters of the political security police, the building as it was when I was there in December.

I projected several disappointing views of the forest interior after sundown. Given the screen at our disposal, the effect was negligible. To induce the trance, I decided to make the order of the slides less haphazard. I showed the Calle 19 de Febrero, the pool where the jacarés were fattened up before being hoisted out by the tail and dragged off to the chopping block by the kitchen. Then a basin, the tortoise pen, the monkey cage. Between the kitchen door and the palisade you could see the courtyard drenched in sunshine and blood.

Night is falling, I said. You're walking the judge toward the ponds of Mapiaupi.

Next slide: railroad tracks running off through the grass and into the trees. There was no path. You had to walk along the tracks. Pomponi and Golpiez heading into the background and the gathering dusk.

Golpiez made banal remarks about the vegetation. I shook him by the shoulder.

Enough, Golpiez! I yelled. You're with Pomponi! That's undeniable! Describe him!

Rather abruptly, I slammed in a photograph of the second courtyard. An interrogator had been immortalized at the moment of inquisition. He was brandishing a machete with the sun at his back, and his face had disappeared into a dazzling halo profaned by his disheveled hair; wiry black strands mingled with the rays of light. It was impossible to determine if he was an underling or one of the high-ranking Auguani thugs.

Pomponi's description, said Golpiez. In his fifties. Indestructible willpower and sense of irony. Hair every which way, as though charged with electricity—sometimes it even seemed to give off sparks. When María Gabriela talked about him, her bust and hips used to quiver voluptuously.

Were they still surucating then? María Gabriela and Pomponi? I asked.

I don't know, replied Golpiez.

Of course you know, Fabianito, murmured Manda. The idea made you sick. You worked hard in the revolution. You had revolutionary attitudes, but it was that idea that obsessed you.

I don't remember anymore, insisted Golpiez.

I showed a slide of the ponds of Mapiaupi, but since

Golpiez wasn't confessing anything new, I took him back to
the kitchen courtyard. The sand sloped gently down to the
pool. A jacaré seven yards long was sunbathing, jaws half-
open, hind legs and tail submerged beneath the delicate
duckweed. A small band of cooks was heading straight for it.
You could also see a suspect waiting over by the palisade, a
Jucapira. Perhaps Golpiez, perhaps me. There was practically no difference between our memories of these interrogations, and I was not thrilled to have to trot them out like
this in public. My hands were shaking.

The projector clicked again.

We were back on the train tracks, in the forest. The ponds
gleamed in the distance, behind the trees. There was an
April moon that night.

So, what about your walk together? I prompted him.

The train was often attacked, said Golpiez. A barricade
would be erected across the tracks and set on fire. The loco-
motive would stop. They didn't mistreat the conductors —
they'd make them get off the train and return to Mapiaupi
on foot. The massacres usually occurred beyond the ponds
of Mapiaupi, a two-hour walk with stretchers. We'd set out to
fetch the wounded at any hour of the day or night, as soon
as news of the killings reached the hospital. The attackers —
whether government soldiers or rebels — never claimed
responsibility for the ambush or explained their motives
and objectives. This kind of information could only be
obtained by carefully questioning any survivors. Interrogators worked alongside the medical personnel. Those questioned were less than cooperative. Despite all evidence to
the contrary, they would deny having seen anything important, or else would provide only incidental information, the
names of the various grasses through which the mutilated
bodies had crawled, for example, or their best guess as to
what time it had been when such and such a bat had flown

screeching overhead in the twilight and then disappeared. The researchers bent over the stretchers. They demolished the suspects' defenses, picked over what had been inaccurately reported. They busied themselves with all that while we were rushing back to the hospital. Often the wounded died along the way.

Exhausted, Golpiez stopped talking. His fever had gone up and he needed to catch his breath.

Don't slow down now, Golpiez! I shouted. You've been avoiding the main issue! I'm still waiting for Pomponi! And stop all that gasping!

I ran slides slowly through the projector. Judge Pomponi speechifying in close-up, medium shot, imperialist shot, strolling with Golpiez beneath the trees, by the ponds, lending Golpiez the pistol he carried as an official of the judiciary. Then we were back in the courtyard again.

The Auguanis surrounded the crocodile, which watched them without understanding, and thus without trembling. Defeating a jacaré demands speed and audacity. Those who do not decapitate their dinner in time, those who hesitate before its jaws, do not survive the battle unscathed. A gigantic, crushing whip lashes suddenly into them.

The interrogator had asked me a question. I'd forgotten what about. Out of the corner of my eye, I was watching the stagnant pool and what the cooks were preparing to do there.

We'd walked over to the ponds at Mapiaupi together several times, said Golpiez, he in his capacity as examining magistrate, I in mine as male nurse, but sometimes we went there just for the pleasure of making our way through the undergrowth, of cutting a path while trying to spot the moon shining through the labyrinth of vines. We'd chat. He'd had a wide experience of life. He would say things in jest, and I can still hear the paternalistic tone of his voice.

We know all that, Golpiez!

I was eager to learn, continued Golpiez. He taught me the vocabulary of the forest. It's to him that I owe my knowledge of the names of the trees, the ants, the monkeys.

You're just rehashing old stuff! I bellowed. Serve us up something new!

The projector clicked and clacked. On the screen at the back of the hut, an Auguani was foaming with rage. You could see part of the Jucapira suspect's wrinkled neck, each crease silvery with sweat, each fold a brackish trickle of anguish. In the next slide, the Jucapira's head was bent, and now you could see my badly sewn-on ear, that outrageously bungled graft.

And speak up! You can see for yourself, what with my ear the way it is . . .

We'd arrived at the ponds, said Golpiez. It's a large open area formed by a succession of broad sheets of water. The moonlight was glancing off all those mirrors. Pomponi was still talking, telling stories about the revolution.

There had been some developments back in the kitchen courtyard. Now there was a huge red patch spread across the bottom of the slide. The layer of duckweed on the pond had been torn in half. The severed head of the jacaré was lying next to me. An Auguani had been hurled over by the tortoise pen, where his corpse lay baking in the sun, with a water lily draped on one leg and another by his left clavicle and the cervical vertebrae, where the skeleton had been most severely damaged. The cooks had just dragged the jacaré's carcass to the kitchen door, gouging out a bloody trail all the way up the slope from the pond. They were preparing to separate the tail from the trunk. The tail is actually the only part that is eaten.

What stories? demanded the Auguani gruffly, pushing me up against the palisade.

All that awful massacre, I murmured. For so little.

Shut up, Golpiez! roared Gutiérrez. You never under-stood a thing about any of it.

The rain drummed overhead. We sat silent and depressed for a few minutes. I went on automatically showing slides.

Isolated trees in the nocturnal landscape.

Pomponi standing at the base of these isolated silhou-ettes with Golpiez, telling him their names.

Then the Calle 19 de Febrero: the judge's assessor dip-ping a machete into a vermilion pool.

Drawing on my chest with the flat of the blade, showing the knives where to cut.

Then Pomponi strutting before Golpiez, revealing little secrets, his role in the guerrilla operations in Yaguatinga, in Mapiaupi, his opposition to this or that assassination, his approval of this or that execution, boasting and reliving past battles.

Pomponi and Golpiez gazing at the still water of the ponds, breathing deeply of the night air.

Then the Auguanis pushing me down onto the blood-soaked sand, making me crawl over to the jacaré's head, laughing, forcing my head between the creature's jaws.

The next slide was a good one: the kitchen courtyard seen through these rows of primitive fangs.

Near the kitchen door, the jacaré's tail; a bit farther off, the trunk, sprawled on its belly.

Then back to the ponds of Mapiaupi. Pomponi lending Golpiez his service revolver, talking to him about firing under cover of darkness, snap firing, indirect fire, dead angles.

You don't understand anything about all that, Golpiez, blurted out Gutiérrez.

And then? I asked, ignoring the interruption.

Then, nothing. I asked Pomponi what the fireflies glimmering around us were called. Araberaba, he told me. Guama, cuissi, muá.

Show the next slide, Golpiez, commanded Gutiérrez.

Back in the headquarters of the political security unit. Someone's head was inside that fetid jacaré head, his cheek lying against its lukewarm tongue. The Auguanis were pressing its jaws together.

A phenomenon often observed after death agonies deep in the forest then took place over by the kitchen. The reptile's trunk roused itself from its coma and seemed to take heart. Deprived of both ends, it nevertheless took off on what it had left, its four legs, moving slowly toward a more dignified inexistence, gushing blood, but making progress, dragging itself instinctively in the right direction, toward the pond, toward the mud.

This was visible through the teeth.

The noise of the storm had died away by the end of the afternoon; because it was so late, the sky cleared without growing lighter. A few birds cheeped nearby. Then we heard a single crystalline note, one drop falling from a great height onto a hard, smooth surface. The birds twittered a bit more.

While we'd been chatting and Golpiez had talked without admitting anything, Manda had died. I don't know exactly when. It was some time before we noticed. She hadn't said anything in particular during the last hour of the session. She'd stayed stretched out on her side, without complaining, moaning unobtrusively. Now she had stopped breathing. Her eyes were glazed.

An orange caterpillar climbed up on her ankle. Gutiérrez picked it off with his thumb and forefinger and flicked it angrily into the bushes. Then he went to sit at the river's edge. His arm stank appallingly. We didn't say anything.

After a minute he asked, without turning around, if amputation was really inevitable. I didn't reply.

Golpiez stroked Manda's hand. Lying prostrate next to her, he confined himself to this simple gesture.

We'll put her in one of the pirogues, I said.

Yes, he agreed. Night is coming on. It's time.

Awkwardly, he caressed her hand.

I flipped over the canoe. Beneath it Gutiérrez had stashed some hunks of snake meat intended for our evening meal. Ants now swarmed over the feast. I hauled the canoe over to where Gutiérrez was sitting.

Need some help, Fabianito? he asked.

I'll manage, I said.

I pushed the canoe into the water. Gutiérrez tried to guide it without using his bad arm, but his body proved recalcitrant and unreliable, so his gymnastics were in vain. The gangrene had affected his entire system and rendered him completely unfit. He kept a morose eye on the canoe floating in front of him, while I went back to the hut.

We had to carry Manda. Golpiez took hold of her under her armpits. Her large and very brown breasts escaped from her dress once again, wobbling with every step we took. I was holding her by the ankles. Over that short distance we lost our balance three times. We'd drop our burden and collapse breathless in the grass, lying on the ground with Manda.

We laid her in the bow of the canoe, as though leaving room on purpose for someone to kneel in the stern to paddle. The craft rocked for a moment but then floated evenly.

We stood in the dying light like gray stumps. Passive.

I thought of Manda, who had been there decade after decade, always available to console us, never influencing our destiny. I thought of Manda, about whom we knew nothing.

Gutiérrez and Golpiez were shivering next to me. It's customary to say a few words. None of us had the strength.

Then Golpiez climbed into the stern of the canoe. I fetched some fruit from the supplies we'd secured in the shelter. I piled the fruit next to Golpiez.

The hut was still visible up on the bank in the gathering darkness, illuminated by the flame in the viewer.

We all shared a feeling of guilt and uneasiness. This went on for half, three-quarters of an hour, with no change. Night had by now invaded the flooded forest. Golpiez did not know how to leave.

Something wriggled at our feet, one of those fish that love to writhe around in extremely shallow water stirring up the slime and plant debris.

Tell me its Indian name, I said.

An arambari, said Golpiez.

No, grumbled Gutiérrez. It's a tamuatá.

Doesn't matter, I said. Give us more names! Keep on naming and don't stop! List all the possibilities!

A jatuarana, stammered Golpiez. A miranha, perhaps? Or an arumaça, a bagre-cangatá? . . . A taiabucu? . . .

Louder! I ordered. Faster! Paddle as you say the names! . . . Paddle faster!

A matupiri! said Golpiez. An uatacupá!

His voice was growing fainter. He was gradually vanishing into the night.

Don't stop! I yelled. Paddle! It's a long list!

Or a gurijuba, an urumaru, a jacunda, recited Golpiez. A jacunda-piranga . . . A guamajacu . . . A jaraquí, a cuacacujá . . .

Can't see him anymore, said Gutiérrez.

From then on, things happened as a matter of course.

At sunrise I noticed the giant guandiras in the treetops.

They looked like big bony lanterns up in the foliage. I hadn't seen them appear the previous evening, and they hadn't betrayed their presence during the night by a single cry, but at first light they were there, already hanging in dreaming position, wrapped in their wings. Motionless. The evidence showed they had spent the night with us. Their excrement was scattered all over our camp.

I extricated myself from my hammock and went to wake Gutiérrez, who opened an eye and asked me how long it would be before we reached Puesto Libertad. I corrected him, reminding him that we had seen the last of Puesto Libertad and that our goal from now on was to go upriver on the Abacau and establish Juaupes, an egalitarian commune governed by a shamanistic and revolutionary administration, and to set up a clinic for the surviving Cocambos and Jabaanas in the area.

Be quiet, Golpiez, he said. You've been mistaken about our objectives from the very beginning.

His pain came and went, bouts of indescribable suffering followed by remissions. I had poured gallons of Cocambo potions into him, and when they began to run out, I went foraging around the camp to find medicines that might act as analgesics. He refused to let out a single moan, from a sense of discipline and heroism. I had bluntly described to him the probable course of his infection and had ruled out the idea of amputation, which at this stage would have been pointless butchery. He begged me not to hack off his arm and simply waited in silence, with exemplary courage, for the limb to fall off.

That night the guandiras must have been hovering over him. There were droppings on his good arm, on his shirt, on the internationalist medal he'd brought along with the iguana hooks and which he'd pinned on his chest with other good-luck talismans. I brushed the dung away and got him back into the pirogue.

I paddled from dawn until late afternoon.

Two days went by like that.

Gutiérrez would lie in the bow, stunned by the flood of herbal painkillers coursing through his veins. I'd slipped thorns from curative plants under his skin, near the medal pinned to his shirt.

When he emerged from his stupor he would tell me— still mistaking me for Golpiez—that we were going to end our journey in a blaze of glory, with a strictly egalitarian community where even the most destitute would be entitled to free psychiatric care, where Jucapiras would be pegged as traitors only after an impartial scrutiny of their files, where Coariguaçus would not be routinely accused of being informers or provocateurs. I always agreed with him heartily, hoping to prolong his euphoria. Sometimes he grew so enthusiastic that he would address the surrounding waters, polishing the speech he intended to make to the assembled Jabaanas and Cocambos to mark the foundation of the commune.

. . . that the lowest of the low should be the undisputed masters . . . absolute . . . that the Cocambos, the Jabaanas should become the masters . . . that they should then eliminate all who hang back . . . make a fresh start in the forest . . . set up internationalist columns . . . march on to victory . . . struggling in the mire for ten years if necessary . . .

I'd answer him, filling out our political debate with enumerations of a floral or faunal theme. Gutiérrez would go back to sleep. He'd vomit and nod off.

We weren't eating anymore. I'd thrown the remains of the snake to the piranhas. In the clearings where we bivouacked, the ripe mangoes had been bitten and spoiled by bats.

We paddled through one channel after another, twisting and turning. All sense of direction soon faded from my mind and the world around me: the four points of the compass brightened together in the morning light, as in those schizophrenic visions Golpiez had. In the distance the trees sometimes contracted into a solid mass. In certain narrow creeks, the water seemed to have been fermenting there for centuries.

There wasn't a trace of Indians anywhere. We heard almost no noise, as though we had suddenly been struck deaf or were crossing a zone contaminated by poison.

We're getting close, said Gutiérrez, without opening his eyes. Can you smell it?

I flared my nostrils. I sat perfectly still. Droplets rolled along the edge of the paddle and plinked into the river below.

So, do you smell it? he asked again. That smoke?

No, I replied.

I didn't want to admit that I'd detected a faint odor, a hint of the smoke belched out by the municipal oil mill of Puesto Libertad.

A hallucination, I said.

You don't know how to sniff things, Golpiez. None of you people can scent properly.

Whom do you mean?

But he had already retreated into unconsciousness.

I began paddling again. I was anxious to get away from there.

I had thus far been spared the ravages of malaria, but later it fell upon me with a vengeance. I could feel the attack coming. In the space of a few minutes my temperature soared and my body became an uncontrollable mass of quivering and rapidly dehydrating flesh. I could hardly draw breath. My head was on fire, burning up on the inside. I lay down in the stern of the canoe. Almost all sound died away, except for the pounding of my own blood.

Debris occasionally drifted down into the craft from the trees, mostly dying spiders or butterflies of unusual size and ugliness. As I watched them fall near or on me, I gasped, I twitched, I dissolved. To exorcise my fear, I pretended my hand was a huge caranguejeira at the point of agony, and even beyond. I'd taught Golpiez the technique of this little hand theater during one of our last sessions in my office, and while I made my fingers dance, I remembered Puesto Libertad, the interrogations, the diapotherapy, the stench of hot metal the projector gave off by the end of the session, the odors of monkeys or crushed and pressed coconuts or crocodilian wallows that drifted in the window at different times during the day, and I saw Golpiez again, saw him sometimes truly hallucinating and sometimes only pretending, taking refuge in a false trance and fake memories so that the hail of questions would not wound him so deeply, inventing memories that coincided with mine, with what he supposed to be my past, or sometimes trying as well to embroil his destiny with that of other revolutionaries like us, retelling in the first person the epic story of Jucapiras who resembled us, identifying with anonymous stomatologists, with internationalist medical orderlies, doctors or shamans similar to us in every way. I sat up on the hammock I'd folded and stowed in the bottom of the canoe; I opened my eyes, brushing from my face the salty streams flowing afresh or growing cold on my cheeks. It took me a minute to realize that my hand was not a spider.

My breath came in spasms.

The odor of the municipal oil mill was not going away.

Daylight was fading without turning into night.

I threw overboard the moribund bodies and leaf litter. Gutiérrez muttered the names in passing. Panapanamuçu the butterfly. We set out again. I was quaking. The paddle weighed a ton.

I wanted to put some distance between us and the stale, ghostly smells of Puesto Libertad. I paddled through the maze of narrow channels. Even fast asleep, I kept on paddling.

At some point, the wailing of Gutiérrez roused me from my torpor. He was leaning overboard, and I thought he was vomiting. Then I understood why he was sobbing. The tendons in his shoulder had snapped. His arm had fallen into the water. Now I leaned overboard, determined to rescue the sinking limb at all costs, throwing every resource into the effort, fishing around with the paddle and the iguana hooks, vainly stammering encouragement at Gutiérrez. Finally I gave up and turned the canoe toward the riverbank.

I could feel the fever returning. In another few minutes I would be burning up again, helpless and delirious.

We'll camp here, I said.

Dejectedly, we looked around at the place where the prow of the canoe had run aground. An open, level place surrounded by trees with brittle gray leaves. The lower branches and undergrowth were covered with gritty dust sheets.

Caranguejeira territory, whispered Gutiérrez.

Doesn't matter, I said. We have to regain our strength. We have to take care of ourselves, Rui. We'll stop here.

When I stepped ashore, my face was immediately swathed in silk. The material was strong and pressed uncomfortably against my lips and eyelids. Horrified, I tore at the skeins of invisible thread all around me, thus alerting the entire colony to my arrival. I heard the whispery rustling in their nests and their soft footfalls nearby as they moved through the grass and between the trees.

Disentangling myself, I climbed back into the canoe and sat down on the damp hammock. Wisps of sticky silk still clung to my hair. My temples were throbbing and sweat was pouring off me again.

We caught sight of a stream glimmering about fifty yards away, behind the trees and the silent snares.

Well, perhaps you're right after all, I said. We'll look for someplace more lively, with Cocambos and Jabaanas. We might try to find our way to the watercourse on the other side of this strip of land.

You don't know what you're talking about, Golpiez, said Gutiérrez. This place is fine. We're going to found the town of Juaupes right here.

Here? I exclaimed. But there's not even a single bird around—there's nothing but spiders!

So what? roared Gutiérrez. Since the Cocambos have gone into hiding . . .

He was kneeling clumsily in the bow of the canoe, trying to keep his balance without his arm. He wanted to manage going ashore on his own.

Since the Jabaanas have refused all our offers! he sputtered. When he stepped intrepidly out of the canoe, I rushed forward to help, but the craft slipped out from under him, and as I reached the bow I was coated with black muck. He had already tumbled into the mud at the water's edge.

I did my best to hoist him back into the canoe, but failed. I went ashore again to try to drag him onto the grass rippling about my ankles and turning gray with silt. Immersed up to his medal and slightly tilted, Gutiérrez flailed about, floundering lopsidedly, maddened by the idea that he was now a one-armed cripple. Moaning and bellowing, he lashed out at the stunted reeds by the shore. He wasn't drowning, for he was standing in semiliquid slime, but he suspected that the unstable bottom beneath his feet was only fooling him and would soon disintegrate, sucking him down. He screamed in fear. I couldn't manage to help him.

Quiet, Golpiez, he said, calming down at last. Leave me. I'm not suffering. Not even morally.

I let go of him. I was exhausted. I climbed painfully back into the canoe and collapsed.

I'm going to explain our plan to them, announced Gutiérrez. Let me do the talking. You wouldn't know how to speak to them.

Them? Who? I asked.

You'd probably frighten them instead, with your Jucapira sermonizing, he added.

In spite of the fever cramps and shaking that left me breathless, I heaved myself up on one elbow to see what he was gazing at with those drug-injected eyes. The shadows were closing in, but an audience had assembled in the lingering daylight: dozens and dozens of caranguejeiras had emerged from their lairs and were studying us, petrified. The Cocambos had always claimed that, deep in the forest, the caranguejeiras organized themselves into communities as advanced as our own but without any hierarchization, or police, or heroes.

A foot offshore, Gutiérrez was croaking, splashing and belching. Sometimes he was quiet. Only his head and upper chest were above the surface. He seemed settled in that viscous water, as though he'd chosen the serenity of an amphibian life for his last hour. He was concentrating. Polishing his address to the masses.

I floated silently nearby. A minute passed, then another. Behind the first curtain of vegetation, the caranguejeiras— for some inconceivable reason dictated by the needs of their commune—had cleared a vast, colorless field across which draperies of saliva had been unfurled everywhere. Walking through such a decor was out of the question, and even my eyes wandered over it only with the utmost prudence. I was trying to get a good look at the river flowing beyond the field.

Quite far off, across the water, a very small light flickered and went out.

There seems to be some kind of house out there, I exclaimed.

Gutiérrez was in no state to reply. He was straining fiercely out of the mud and had already stuck out his clenched fist in true oratorical fashion, prepared to hammer home his ideas, as well as the clumps of grass that would serve as his lectern.

I glimpsed new tiny lights across the river. It was too dark to guess how far away they were, but it was quite clear where they were: the outline they revealed corresponded, on the whole, to that of the slums of Manuela Aratuípe.

I was too feverish to think about this and suddenly wanted only to sleep, but Gutiérrez had begun his speech to the spiders about the revolution, and it was not a lullaby.

. . . that the lowest of the low should be the undisputed masters . . . absolute . . . that they should then eliminate all who hang back . . . those who do not want to live with them in the heart of the forest . . . such is the price of revolution . . . make a fresh start in the forest . . . march on to victory . . . struggling in the mire for ten years if necessary . . . fifty years . . . the Cocambos and the Jabaanas should stop running away and become the masters . . .

. . . not give in to pain . . . to one's own pain . . . ensuring a crushing victory for everyone . . . even if everyone has perished or given up the struggle . . . making a fresh start even all alone . . . even if all the rest have fled . . . must round them up and reinspire them . . . convince them by setting an example, by violence if necessary . . . abolishing inequality . . . so that nothing and no one shall rise above . . . the lowest common denominator . . . proclaiming equality even with only a single voice . . . even stuck in the mud . . . a

166 | ANTOINE VOLODINE

proclamation expressed in the language of the most destitute among us . . . even if they have all disappeared . . . forcing this language to live . . . learning it even when all alone
in the forest . . . speaking it . . .

The small crowd of caranguejeiras had formed a semicir-
cle. On branches, in bushes, at times rocking back and forth
beneath their canopies of silk, they listened without hostility
or interest. They were putting in an appearance.

I disagreed with Gutiérrez on a few points of his pro-
gram, but these were minor objections that I kept to
myself. I did not abandon Gutiérrez; I nodded approval of
his conclusions, encouraged him to keep up his momen-
tum, and finished words or sentences for him when his
voice faltered. If a pause dragged on too long while he
tried to catch his breath or organize his thoughts, I felt it
my duty to show my support for him and the revolution in
general, so I stepped into the breach, thus affirming in no
uncertain terms that I was an integral part of the perfor-
mance. I kept our audience entertained, dramatizing the
appropriate behavior with my fingers, acting out an egalitarian way of stretching little legs, settling down, and waiting patiently.

Night had fallen. Gutiérrez went on speaking.

. . . must level down to the lowest common denominator
to begin with . . . let those who stand out humble themselves . . . speaking the language of those who are forgotten . . . of those who have been killed . . . of those who no
longer exist . . .

I followed Gutiérrez's harangue for a long time, until my
fever rose again and burned my mind to cinders, so that I
never knew how his speech ended, with what stirring
appeals and on which hopeful note. Our listeners had vanished, one by one. Now the canoe was drifting, carrying me

away from where Gutiérrez raved on, perhaps, or wavered, hesitating. The craft bumped into a root.

The night fell silent. I opened my eyes. Listless clouds obscured the stars. I could not see much of anything, except the faint, sporadic twinkling, far beyond the spiders' field, of the shantytown called Manuela Aratuípe.